FLIGHT FROM FEAR

The glamorous redhead hired private detective Joe Wayne to escort her to Ashbury, a town fifty miles away. She was frightened, Wayne saw, but she refused to tell him the source of her fear, and when their car crashed and the girl was killed, Wayne had a real problem on his hands. He endeavoured to build up the rough outline of a murder pattern, only to discover that it made no sense. A vital part of the picture was missing and a lot more ground would have to be covered before the true pattern emerged.

RAY OWEN

FLIGHT FROM FEAR

Complete and Unabridged

LINFORD
Leicester

First published in Great Britain by
Robert Hale Limited
London

First Linford Edition
published 2005
by arrangement with
Robert Hale Limited
London

British Library CIP Data

Owen, Ray
Flight from fear.—Large print ed.—
Linford mystery library
1. Detective and mystery stories
2. Large type books
I. Title
823.9'14 [F]

ISBN 1–84617–037–0

Published by
F. A. Thorpe (Publishing)
Anstey, Leicestershire

Set by Words & Graphics Ltd.
Anstey, Leicestershire
Printed and bound in Great Britain by
T. J. International Ltd., Padstow, Cornwall

This book is printed on acid-free paper

1

One look at the girl behind the steering wheel of the car told Joe Wayne two things about her. She was a glamorous redhead and she was dead.

During the next thirty seconds something to do with the girl tumbled around in Wayne's head, and he tried to tie it down. It was like trying to catch a butterfly on the wing with a pin. His brains were so much cotton wool — just like his mouth — and his memory seemed to be out somewhere, visiting relations, maybe.

After another look at the girl his stomach telegraphed a frantic message. Wayne crawled to the door of the car to reach air. Most cars had two doors at least; the car that Wayne was in with the redhead didn't have a door where he was heading.

He tumbled through and found himself in a pile of rocks and weeds, hot and odorous in the copper sunlight.

He never knew how long he lay there: ten seconds perhaps, ten minutes. The sickness passed finally and left room for a different sensation to grip his stomach — fear. Raw and stark.

It brought Wayne out in a cold sweat. He shook himself and attempted to get to his feet. He fell down and cursed softly. He got up again and this time managed to force his legs to remain beneath him.

His head throbbed: it felt as big as two heads at least. There was a cut too. There must be a cut, for blood trickled from his left eyebrow and distorted his sight. He wiped it away and looked at the car.

The car was a fresh job. It had been a fresh job an hour ago. Or was it a year?

Panic hit him when he couldn't remember. It was a Dodge, two-tone, brown and cream. The reason it had no door where Wayne scrambled out was because the door was lying six yards off, shiny and crumpled, spraywork splintered, window shattered.

He noticed something else missing from the Dodge, the near-side front wheel. It had travelled a good deal farther than the car. It was perched in a cleft in the rocks where it must have rolled and bounced to that height before being trapped there. On three wheels the car never had a chance, not in this terrain.

When the initial shock had passed, Wayne's mind began to function. Not lucidly. He found he couldn't concentrate on any definite thought pattern. There simply wasn't any pattern there.

Desperately he burrowed into his memory to find an answer to the problem. Calling it a problem was an understatement.

'I must be going nuts. I must have wrecked my thinking machine in the crash. Who is the dame? How did I happen to be in the car with her? Why did the car leave the road?'

Wayne looked around him then. He could see a fence on a bend where the Dodge had lost the wheel and rocketed through. The fence was shattered at that point. The road was some two hundred yards off. Over here was nothing but rocks, weeds and sand. The murmur of distant water reached his ears. The sea. This must be the Ashbury road out of Darton City. He and the girl must have been driving away from Darton City.

Where the car had finished up it was hidden from the view of any motorist passing along the road. He tried to get a picture.

He and the girl had been driving towards Ashbury. The Dodge had been going into the bend when the wheel parted company with its hub. Strange.

As he stared at the fence again a car rushed from the direction of Darton City. Wayne held his breath. The car went past.

He shuddered and felt in his pockets for cigarettes. He put one in his lips and lit it. His fingers trembled.

He knew who he was. Joe Wayne, private investigator. He had his office in the Wilton Buildings. He had a secretary called Maggie Yarmon. That was it! Maggie would be able to sort the puzzle out for him. The sooner he got in touch with Maggie the better. Memory of this was bound to come back soon. He hoped.

But what about the crashed Dodge and

the redhead who was dead behind the wheel?

The cigarette had calmed him somewhat, cleared a lot of the wool from his brain. Now it was able to spell trouble. Now too it could spell danger.

He moved back to the car and forced himself to look at the dead girl. She *had* been good-looking. She *had* been glamorous. She was dressed in a lightweight two-piece tweed outfit. Her red hair was spilled over her shoulders and down one side of her face. Her eyes were wide open, frozen in a terrible stare. Her handbag lay on the floor at her feet.

Wayne's fingers snatched at the handbag. He brought it to the light and opened it. A cheap cigarette case, an embroidered handkerchief, a silver-plated lighter. Wayne probed and fingered out a roll of bills, fives and tens. He made a rough count. Five hundred dollars at least. A scrap of paper fell and he pounced on it. '*Joseph Wayne*' he read. '*Wilton Buildings*.' His office number was noted too.

Sweat mingled with the blood trickling

from his eyebrow. He pushed the scrap of paper into his pocket, continued searching for identification.

The girl's driving licence was in the bottom of the purse and he read it eagerly. The girl's name was Mitzi Laverick. Her address was given as 412, Comstock Avenue, Darton City.

'Mitzi Laverick . . . Mitzi! Mitzi!'

It didn't ring a bell. It didn't even create a ripple on the stagnant surface of his memory.

He was returning the articles and money to the handbag when a card fell out. Wayne lifted it and glanced at it. It carried Morton Cotter's name and address. That rang a bell right enough. Mort Cotter was a big thing in nightclubs, fun houses. Wayne pushed the card into his pocket with the scrap of paper.

He would have to get out of here, and fast. Newspaper headlines screamed at him.

PRIVATE EYE IN DEATH CAR WITH GIRL! JOSEPH WAYNE BEING HELD BECAUSE OF CRASH MYSTERY!

He was stumbling away when another part of his mind began to function. How could a wheel have come off the car?

Why did any wheel come off a car?

It mustn't have been fitted properly, he realised. It was no time to ponder on the carelessness of garage mechanics. The sooner he climbed off the spot he was on the healthier would be his future.

Nevertheless, curiosity overcame him and he went back to have a look at the car hub. He bent and cuffed sweat from his forehead as he stared at the studs that should have held the wheel in place. The studs had been tampered with. A file had been used on them.

This wasn't an accident at all. This was murder.

He reached the road and began walking. His ribs hurt on his left side and every step he took sent a dull throbbing pain bouncing through his skull. A dozen cars swept past him during the next twenty minutes. None of them stopped; none of their drivers bothered to look at him.

When he saw the roadside café he

almost shouted out in relief. By this time he was sweating all over. His shirt clung to him like a wet rag. Sweat streamed from his face. He halted and looked at the trucks parked on the asphalt yard. The drivers would be inside, eating, drinking coke or coffee. His stomach cried out for a drink of coffee.

He was heading on to the door when he halted again and fumbled a handkerchief from his pocket. He wiped his face and forehead with it. The bleeding had eased off, but he must look a sight. He edged on to the window and tried to catch his reflection in the glass. He didn't think it looked so bad. There were a few cars parked too and nobody would know but that he had left his car outside.

He entered the café and was hit with a mixture of smells. Air-conditioning was at work, but it needn't have bothered for all the good it was doing. A jukebox blared from a corner. The truck jockeys were together at a table, talking and eating. At other tables lonely men sat and ate quietly, minding their own business. A fat man whistled to the tune from the jukebox as he fixed food at a serving hatch.

Wayne looked around him and saw the phone booth. He walked boldly to it and shut himself in. A thought occurred to him and he glanced at his wristwatch. It said ten after three. He held it to his ear to make sure it hadn't stopped. Maggie would be in the office. He brought out money and picked what he needed.

Maggie Yarmon's sharp voice was like a breath of fresh air.

'Wayne Investigations here!'

'Maggie, this is me . . . '

'Joey! What the hell *are* you playing at? I thought . . . '

'Never mind what you thought. Did I leave the car there?'

'Did you — Look, what's the matter with you anyhow? Have you lost your memory or something?'

Wayne fought for patience, resisted the urge to bawl Maggie out for a stupid so and so.

'Did I leave the car there?'

'Yeah! Sure you did. Where are you? Has somebody knocked the car off?'

'Cut the cackle, Maggie. Just listen to me. Do you understand?'

'Yeah . . . ' Maggie sounded mildly concerned. 'Go ahead, Joey. I'm getting you fine.'

'Lock up the office and get into the car. Come out here as fast as you can. Is that clear?'

'You must be kidding. I might be efficient at lots of things, Joey, but I'm no clairvoyant. Out where?'

Wayne opened the door of the booth as a couple of truckers headed from the café.

'What's the name of this joint?'

'Is that supposed to be a joke, Mac?'

'No. I'm serious. I'm putting a call through . . . '

'Rich Pace's Pie Parlour,' the trucker said.

'Much obliged.' Wayne shut himself off again. 'Pace's Pie Parlour,' he told Maggie.

'And the same to you,' Maggie Yarmon said. 'What do you take me for? You're stoned, pal.'

Wayne seethed.

'Do what I tell you or draw your time,' he snarled. 'Bring the car to Pace's Pie Parlour on the Ashbury road. I'll be watching out for you.'

'All right, Joey,' Maggie said resignedly. 'You're the boss. But I'm telling you, you're stoned.'

Wayne hung up and went over to the counter. He asked the trim brunette for a highball. The brunette let her eyelashes flutter at him.

'You've wandered into the wrong store, mister. Coffee, tea, coke, milk. No highball. I'm sorry. Did somebody hit you on the head?'

'Forget it,' Wayne told her. Mention of his head reminded him that it was throbbing. 'Coffee. Make it strong, No sugar. No cream.'

'I wouldn't dream of it,' the girl responded. She began to take an interest in Wayne. 'Hot, ain't it?'

'Hot,' Wayne said. It seemed his brains were trying to break out of his skull.

The coffee was set out and he paid. Something fell from the hand he had gathered the money in. It hit the counter and fell on the other side. The girl stooped to lift it, glancing at the card before she reached it back.

'Private investigator? I hope you don't think I'm nosey.'

'I thing you're cute,' Wayne growled. He rammed the calling card into his pocket. It shouldn't have been lying around loose in his pocket; it should have been in his wallet.

He carried the coffee to a table and began to sip. When he looked at the counter the brunette was smiling at him.

'Elsie!' the fat man at the serving hatch called. 'Steak sandwiches coming up.'

'Keep your skin on.'

Wayne swallowed the coffee and left the café. Outside, the sun seemed to be waiting for him. It hit him between the eyes with everything it had and he blinked. He lit a cigarette and began walking about.

What the hell was keeping Maggie, he wondered.

Ten minutes slid past by his watch. Time enough for somebody using the Ashbury road to be curious enough about the broken fence to stop and look.

Wayne needed a drink, a real drink. He needed his head to stop travelling in circles. He was lighting another cigarette when the Plymouth turned off the road and halted.

Maggie Yarmon stuck her head out.

'What are you waiting for — somebody to give you a roll of drums?'

He staggered on his way to the car. This close Maggie Yarmon noticed and bounded out to catch his arm.

'You and your hot-blooded broads,' she snarled. 'See what they do for you. You ought to be ashamed of yourself. What did she hit you with?'

'Who?' Wayne pleaded as he dropped down on the passenger seat. 'Maggie, I — '

His secretary appeared to recede and vanish and he never finished what he intended saying.

When he opened his eyes he was at home in his apartment on Vine. Maggie was fussing like a hen over a chick that had gone out in the rain. She was placing a cold compress on his brow and it felt good to Wayne.

'How did I get here?'

'You can bet you didn't walk it. I got the janitor to help tote you to the elevator. I told him you were stoned . . . '

'Quit saying I'm stoned.'

'Then you're nuts,' Maggie told him. There was something suspiciously like a tear in her eye. She forced a glass into his hand and wrapped his fingers round it.

'What is it?'

'Cyanide. Eighty proof. Drink it up. I said I would give you two more minutes, then I'd get a sawbones. I still think I ought to get a sawbones. Some of your bolts are loose.'

'I'm okay.'

'You just think! You've got a lump on your head would do for practising mountain climbing. You look green. You've had some kind of concussion. Don't try to talk. Don't go away — '

'Where do you think you're going?'

'Only as far as the phone. I'm gonna get a doc.'

'You're gonna get a kick in your silk-trimmed pants if you try.'

14

'But Joey. It could be serious. I was going to call that dame you play around with. Fanny what's-her-name . . . '

'If you're talking about Ruth you can forget that too,' Wayne told her. He drank from the glass. It was scotch with all the stops pulled. It seemed to do things to Wayne's perspective.

Suddenly he thought of Mitzi Laverick and sprang up from the couch. The pain hit him and put him down again.

'Now I remember!' he cried.

'Don't strain it, Joey. Whatever in hell you do, don't strain it. I heard of a guy was concussed, and you know what happened to him . . . '

'Somebody murdered her, Maggie,' Wayne panted.

'Take it easy, Joe,' Maggie warned. 'The guy I heard about had them too.'

'Had what, damn it?'

'Hallucinations. You see things you wouldn't look at if you were in your right mind. Sometimes it happens in Technicolor. This guy had to go to a — '

'Knock it off, Maggie! I'm not nuts. I'm not stoned. That knock on the head

15

must have triggered off a mild amnesia.'

'Come again,' Maggie said. 'You do have a lump on your skull. Somebody could have knocked you over the head. Somebody did hit you over the head. That dame. I warned you. She had green eyes and red hair. You should never try to rape a dame with green eyes and red hair. Didn't anybody ever tell you the facts of life, Joey?'

'Her name was Mitzi Laverick.'

'She had green eyes and red hair.'

'Oh, the hell with her green eyes and red hair! Look what you're making me say, Maggie. You shouldn't talk ill of the dead. Dead! Dead!'

Wayne sat up on the edge of the couch. The pain hit him again, but not so heavily this time. He emptied the scotch in the glass, held the glass to Maggie.

'Fill it up.'

'But, Joey — '

'Fill it up, Maggie. You'd better fill one up for yourself too.'

'Not me. No sir! Right now I don't like the looks of you at all, Joe. You've got a kinda green look in your eye too. I've been a virgin for a long time, and — '

'Listen, sweet dreams,' Wayne grated. 'I wouldn't assault you if you were the last woman on earth. You're old enough to be my maiden aunt. You've got a face like the back of a bus. Besides which — '
He broke off when Maggie chuckled.

'What did I say wrong?'

'Not a thing, Joey. You've just come back into tune. I figured you'd never be normal again. I'll fix you another drink for sure. One for myself if you want a maudlin office help on your hands. But one thing you've got to promise me you'll do, pal.'

'What?' Wayne demanded hoarsely.

'Come down from cloud nine and tell the truth for a change. A dead dame indeed! What kind of yarn will you try to drum up next to spring on me?'

Wayne groaned.

He wondered if the whole thing had really happened in his head after all.

2

It was a motorcycle cop who noticed the smashed fence on the bend of the Ashbury road. He brought his machine in to the side and killed the engine. Then he dismounted and traced the tyre marks from the road to the gap in the fence. Broken wood was everywhere. It was very hot and the cop took a handkerchief from a hip pocket to pat at his brow.

He stood on tiptoes to try and get a better view of the rocks over there. Some bum had taken the corner too fast and gone into a skid. Serve him right too, if he was that careless of his life and limb. By the looks of things he must have recovered and made it back to the road again.

The cop decided he would love to get his hands on the guy.

He was turning from the view of rocks and weeds and sand when something over there reflected the sunlight and blinded him momentarily.

'For pete's sake!'

The cop left the road hurriedly and scrambled through the rocks until he had a view of the car. He went faster now, wondering if someone was hurt and trapped in the wreck.

When he was close enough to the Dodge to see the redhead behind the wheel his breath whistled from his teeth. He was a big man and his activity from the road had really brought the sweat to his pores. One look was enough to tell him the girl was dead. He checked her neck for pulse-beat all the same. There was no pulse-beat. Body temperature was practically zero. The cop judged that the girl had been dead for around thirty minutes.

A swift, embracing glance showed him the door that had been wrenched from the Dodge in the crash, the front wheel that had come away from the Dodge and likely caused the accident. The wheel struck a queer note. A flat he could see through; he couldn't understand the wheel coming off.

He had seen enough to go on with and made his way back to the motorcycle. He radioed headquarters, and when Communications answered, 'Lashlin here. Listen. I'm on the Ashbury road out of town. There's been a bad accident at the bend just above Pace's Pie Parlour. Dame in a Dodge. Car wrecked. Dame dead.'

The report was okayed. Lashlin wiped his brow again. A car slowed on the curve and the driver looked at the cop and on to the fence. The face was vaguely familiar to Lashlin.

'Anything the matter, Officer?'

'Yeah,' Lashlin grunted grudgingly. He didn't care for rubber-necks. 'Keep moving, will you?'

'Car go through the fence?'

'Damn right. Driver dead.'

'Can I help?' the guy asked. He was swarthy and had very black eyes.

'Just keep moving, is all.'

'Whatever you say, Officer.'

The car picked up speed and drove off towards Ashbury. The cop lit a cigarette and left his motorcycle. He returned to the accident scene. That wheel coming off stuck in his mind. He knew enough about cars to ask himself questions.

At the Dodge he had another look at the redhead, just to make sure. There was no possible doubt she was dead. She was a swell looker too. The car had state plates. Lashlin dragged his gaze from the staring eyes. A hell of a way to end up, he reflected.

He saw the handbag and lifted it, noticing the money, the knick-knacks. He opened the licence and read it. So the girl was a local. He left the handbag where he'd found it, then stooped to have a look at the wheel hub.

'Holy cow! The wheel has been tampered with. Somebody meant this baby to have a smash-up . . . '

He met Sergeant Hank Peterson when two official cars and an ambulance raced into the bend and stalled. Excitement lent a high note to his voice.

'That doesn't look like an accident at all, Sarge. The wheel studs were cut with a file. Somebody must have wanted to murder the dame.'

The gaunt-featured Petersen went

carefully to the scene, followed by other officers, the ambulance crew, and a medical examiner who had come along as a matter of course.

When he had checked on the girl and the wheel hub he snapped at one of the officers.

'Put a call in for the lab gang, Sutters. The rest of you spread out and start searching. She may have had a companion in the car. Lashlin, you don't have to hang around. You didn't see the actual crash?'

'The dame has been dead half an hour at least, Sarge,' Lashlin said meaningly. He was rewarded with twin spots of colour in Petersen's cheeks.

'You didn't touch anything?'

'Just to check she was dead. Then to check who she was with her handbag.'

'Okay. I'll take over from here.'

'Here's a cigarette butt, Sarge,' an officer announced and extended it in the palm of his hand.

'Yeah!' Petersen took it in the palm of his own hand and studied it. Then he sniffed it. 'Fresh. Chesterfield.' He went over to the car and looked at the redhead. The interns were waiting for the lab crew to get busy before taking the body away. The medical examiner was finished with it for the moment. The redhead wore a pale crimson lipstick.

'Is that stuff kiss-proof?'

'What a morbid idea, Sarge!'

'Knock it off.' Petersen produced a white handkerchief and wrapped part of it round his index finger. He leaned forward and touched the open mouth with it. The result was a faint crimson smear.

Now he opened the ashtray and saw a lot of butts. All of them were faintly stained with the crimson lipstick. Next he brought the girl's handbag to the light and checked the contents. The cigarette case he examined and brought out a cigarette. Camels.

He turned to the watching faces.

'She could have had a passenger. Spread out like I told you and keep searching. If she had a guy in the car he could be wandering around with a hole in his head. Where's the nearest gas station?'

'There's a diner along the road, Sarge.

We passed it on the way here. Want me to — '

'No. Let it ride.'

A search of a wide area surrounding the scene produced nothing to interest Petersen. He spent some time studying the door of the car that had come adrift and the wheel wedged in the rocks. The tyre was rock hard. The wheel wasn't buckled in any way.

Who had filed the studs so that the wheel would run off at the first sharp bend?

Lieutenant Floyd Eckert came out with the lab technicians. Another car brought press men, eager for whatever story was going.

'What do you think, Sergeant?' Haggarty of the *Chronicle* demanded. 'Are you treating it as murder?'

'Go away,' Eckert scowled. 'If you touch anything I'll have your hides.'

'That's what we like about you, Lieutenant — your psychology.'

'Punks,' Eckert muttered to Petersen. Eckert had a calm face, alert blue eyes. They swept over the scene. 'What do you make of it?'

'It's murder all right. We'd better sew this up real tight until we get a lead.'

'So you haven't got one? Who was she?'

'Mitzi Laverick. About five hundred bucks in her purse. A nice car. Her clothes aren't that expensive. Nor her shoes, her handbag.'

'Uhuh! That makes a smell?'

'I don't know. You taking over, Lieutenant?'

'Are you sick or something?'

'I'm fine,' Petersen said sharply.

Eckert's eyes twinkled briefly. 'Carry on. You've got a couple of clues. A picture of her background should add some more.'

'She had a passenger.'

Eckert glared at him.

'Who? Where? Do you want to keep it a secret?'

Petersen showed him the cigarette butt. 'A guy was smoking this not long ago.'

'A guy. How come?'

'No lipstick. The dame has. The butts in the ashtray have. He could have wandered off.'

'He could have jumped a split second before the car crashed,' Eckert said.

Petersen hadn't thought of that. He nodded.

'That could be the killer.'

'The boys with the microscopes might find prints. This could be good, Hank. Okay. Spread yourself. Have what you need.'

'Thanks,' Petersen said drily.

He walked through the rocks to the road and got into one of the cars. Lieutenant Eckert hurried after him.

'Where are you going?'

'I figured to get something on the passenger maybe.'

'Where?' Eckert persisted. He stared suspiciously at Petersen, thinking he had something in his head he was trying to keep to himself.

'Pace's Pie Parlour. It's just a chance. I'd like to have this road combed from here to town and from here to Ashbury.'

'I'll take care of it, Hank. I wouldn't be too hopeful.'

It was hot in the car and Petersen put the air-conditioning to work. He cruised in at the front of Pace's café and parked. He stood at the door and got a cigarette to his lips. A few truckers, he saw. Nothing much else.

The fat man had heard of the car crash and came away from the serving hatch when he spotted the newcomer. His eyes ran over Petersen, guessing what he was.

'They say there's a wreck along the road?'

'That's right. Look — ' Petersen dropped his voice. 'What kind of trade do you have here — mixed, regulars?'

'Mostly regulars. The truckers like the grub. So do a lot of strangers though.'

'I see. Give me a cup of coffee.'

The fat man brought it himself. Petersen moved to a table and the fat man took it over. He sat down opposite the policeman and hooked thick fingers together.

'Are you looking for somebody? You're police, aren't you?'

'I'm police,' Petersen said. 'I might be looking for somebody. Did you notice many strangers during the last half hour or so?'

'We got a few. Maybe half a dozen.'

'None of them seemed to be hurt? Excited? You know, anything like that.'

'Wait a minute! There was that guy that Elsie served . . . '

'Elsie?' Petersen eyed the trim brunette back of the counter. 'Are you Pace?'

'Rich Pace,' the fat man said. 'That's me.'

'Send Elsie over, Rich.'

'She don't like cops. A cop set her up one time. She nearly sued for breach of promise.'

'She'll like me,' Petersen told him with a smile. 'I won't spring anything nasty on her.'

Petersen took a sip from his cup while he waited. The brunette stared at him while Rich Pace talked. She flushed a little and came round the counter. Petersen noticed that she had very nice legs. She stood and looked at him until he smiled and asked her to sit down.

'I won't take a bite out of you.'

'I'll believe you when you don't,' came the quick retort. 'You're asking about some guy . . . '

'He might have been a passenger in a car that went through the fence along the road. He might have been dazed, hurt. Did you notice anybody that made you look twice?'

'Say, now when you mention it! A fellow did come in. Used the phone, then came over and asked for a highball — '

'Go on,' Petersen urged when she broke off. 'Anything else you remember?'

'He bought a cup of coffee. When he paid he dropped a card on the counter. It fell to the floor and I picked it up. He snapped it from me. He was some kind of investigator . . . '

'Insurance?'

'Private, the card said. He had a lump on his head that was bleeding a little.'

'Did you notice his name?' Petersen asked eagerly.

The brunette's face fell.

'I'm sorry.'

'Never mind,' Petersen grinned. He was disappointed, but he had learned something. 'What did the fellow look like — tall, short? Sandy, bald?'

'He was a nice guy. The type that might

get fresh if he had half a chance.'

Petersen thanked her and left the café. He stood in the sun and poked at his chin with a finger tip.

'A private investigator. I just wonder . . . '

Petersen went into the café again and shut himself in the phone booth. He had forgotten Joe Wayne's number, but he could find it in the book. He found it and dialled. Nobody answered the call. Petersen hung up and got a cigarette going. He frowned at his reflection.

'You're nuts,' he said. 'Joe Wayne wouldn't get himself mixed up in anything of that nature.'

He called Wayne's apartment on Vine all the same. He caught his breath when a female answered.

'Yeah! What do you want?'

'Joe Wayne. Is Joe Wayne there?'

'What do you want?'

'I want Joe Wayne. Is he there? Is that a record or something?'

'Who's asking?'

Petersen winced. Wayne's battleaxe of a secretary. At home in Wayne's apartment.

The detective's mouth twisted up grimly.

'Listen, sister, he is or he isn't. Forget it. I'll ride there and see.'

'No! Hold on ... Mr. Wayne is indisposed at the minute. He — he's in the shower.'

'He'll be out of it by the time I call.'

'No! That's where you're wrong. Lookit, why not see Mr. Wayne at his office in the morning?'

'Why can't I see him now?'

'Because I say so. That's why. Do you want to make something out of it?'

'Okay, honey,' Petersen drawled. 'Have it any way you want it. Be seeing you.'

'At the office in the morning,' Maggie Yarmon said hurriedly. 'We need all the business we can get.'

'I just bet. Be sure and dry behind Wayne's ears when he comes out of the shower.'

Floyd Eckert was waiting for Petersen when he left the café once more. Eckert had a cigarette in his mouth and a glint of suspicion still in his eye.

'Who were you calling?'

'Just somebody.'

'I figured you were working on the case.'

'I am working on the case.'

'You heard something in there?'

'Not a damn thing.'

'Let me try.'

The lieutenant was brushing past him to the door of the café when Petersen caught his arm. Eckert's gaze travelled slowly from the thin man's hand, along his arm to his face.

'Why are you burning?'

'I'm not burning.'

'Why can't I go in there if I want to?'

Petersen released his grip. He looked guilty. He shrugged his shoulders.

'Yeah,' he admitted sheepishly. 'I got a tip.'

Eckert stared at him for a minute without speaking. Now Petersen really did begin to burn.

'It's only an idea I have. I don't want to ring any bells until I check it out.'

'Nobody's stopping you,' Eckert smiled. 'Go ahead and check it out.'

'The car might be needed.'

'There's plenty of transport. If we need

more we can get it easily enough. The taxpayers will never hear about it.'

Petersen couldn't trust himself to reply. He said okay and walked to the car he had taken. Behind the wheel he glanced back at the café. Eckert was standing there, hands on his hips. He nodded encouragingly and Petersen drove off.

Eckert noted that he headed back towards town.

He flung his cigarette away and went into the café. He jerked a finger at Rich Pace and didn't make any bones of his mission.

'My man was in here asking questions. What did you tell him?'

'Try Elsie. She knows.'

'Come here, Elsie.'

The brunette was tiring of the limelight and her expression conveyed as much to the lieutenant. Eckert smiled warmly at her.

'What did you tell the guy just left?'

'Why should I tell you? Who are you anyway?'

'I might be Little Bo Peep. I'm not.' Eckert showed her his identification. 'My man got himself mixed up with your information. Tell it to me, please. I'll take a cup of coffee while you talk. Cream, but no sugar.'

He lit another cigarette while he waited. It was very hot, he thought. He wondered vaguely if Hank was getting himself ideas about promotion.

3

'Now you're up a pole,' Maggie Yarmon said. She fixed Joe Wayne with his fourth cup of coffee and took a chair opposite the couch where Wayne sat. Wayne didn't look too good. Which was because he didn't feel too good. 'And they'll likely have me as an accessory after the fact,' Maggie went on. 'Can they do that to me?'

'They might if you don't show enough of your leg.'

'You let her lead you along the garden path,' Maggie continued. She lifted a cup of coffee for herself and took a sip from it. She poked a cigarette at her lips and lit it. She puffed fiercely and eyed Wayne accusingly. 'Why did she want to go to Ashbury anyhow?'

'I told you. She wanted to leave town. She thought she needed protection to get out of town.'

'Then she wasn't kidding, was she?'

Maggie snorted. 'You don't suppose she wanted to commit suicide and needed company to keep her courage up? Joey, did you really lose your memory just then, or are you holding something back I ought to hear?'

Wayne made a gesture of impatience. His skull throbbed where Maggie had applied a strip of Band-Aid.

'You'd better take a powder. If that was Hank Petersen, like you think it was, he'll be here shortly.'

'Meaning the cops have got onto the crash?'

'Meaning nothing else,' Wayne rejoined. 'Run along now while the going's good.'

'I'm not going anywhere. I'm sitting right here until the cops arrive. According to you, this is murder. Okay. You were there when it happened. You were practically holding the dame's hand when the car crashed. Were you holding the dame's hand when the car crashed?'

A hard ring on the doorbell saved Wayne from having to provide an answer.

'Keep your lips sewed,' he warned Maggie Yarmon.

Maggie paused on her way to the door of the apartment. 'What are you going to tell him?'

'The truth.'

Maggie's brows arched slightly while she thought it over. She nodded slowly.

'A good idea maybe. They won't believe you, Joey. They never do. I'm not even sure I believe you myself.'

The bell rang again. The pressure was kept up until Maggie opened the door on Hank Petersen.

'Why, hello, Sergeant. Imagine meeting you here.'

'Just imagine,' Petersen said. He edged past the woman to get into the room. His eyes narrowed on Wayne's face, the cup of coffee in his hand.

'Hello, Hank.'

'Hello, yourself.'

Petersen picked a chair and sat down. He drew the legs of his pants up carefully and crossed them. Maggie closed the door and offered the detective a drink. She tried to catch Wayne's eye but Wayne evaded her glance.

'I could do with a beer, Miss Yarmon. Thanks.'

'Don't mention it.'

Petersen fingered for cigarettes while Maggie went to the kitchen for a can. He made a display of having lost or mislaid his cigarettes. Wayne threw a pack across and Petersen's mouth tightened.

'I rang your office.'

'What's the matter, Hank? You need help on something?'

'Did you have an accident?' Petersen countered.

Wayne eyed him coolly. 'Do you plan to investigate it?'

Petersen took the beer from Maggie before answering. He had a long pull, appreciating its coolness. He nodded and tipped the rest of the can's contents into his glass.

'I'm giving you a chance to talk about it, Joe.'

'And *you* think *you're* smart!' Maggie Yarmon said with a faint sneer.

'Keep out of it, Maggie,' Wayne snapped.

'He lost his memory.'

'What!' Hank Petersen ejaculated softly.

'I told you to button your lip . . . Okay, Hank, you're talking about the Dodge on the Ashbury road?'

'I'm talking about the Dodge on the Ashbury road,' Petersen agreed grimly.

'Were you a passenger in the car?'

'Just watch him, Joey! The way he says it he half suspects you of doing away with the dame. If I were you I wouldn't say another word until I got my lawyer.'

Petersen looked mildly embarrassed.

'Do you want to get your lawyer, Joe?'

Wayne's laugh was a harsh snort. 'Of course not. I intended making a clean breast of everything — '

'Was she a client, by any chance?'

'She was.'

'You knew her name?'

'Her name was Mitzi Laverick.'

'That all?'

'What do you mean, Hank?'

Petersen lifted his shoulders. He pretended to ignore the ominous nearness of Wayne's secretary. He spoke patiently.

'What did she work at?'

'I couldn't say.'

'Okay. But she hired you. She was your client. You were in her car when it crashed. Tell me about that.'

'She wanted me to ride to Ashbury with her. She lived in Darton City, but she planned on moving to Ashbury. I think she planned on moving farther afield when she arrived.'

'What made you think so?'

'I — I don't know.'

Petersen's narrow lips took a downward slant. Grey chill came into his eyes.

'Come off it, Joe. We heard a short time ago. A motorcycle cop spotted the broken fence and investigated. He found the car and the dame. He called it an accident. When he had a better look he changed his verdict to murder.' Petersen raised a hand when Wayne opened his mouth. 'Before you say another word, Joe, I want this straight. I don't mind admitting it looks queer to me. Eckert wants me to handle it. He always hopes I'll yell Uncle to give him a chance to thump his chest. He hasn't thumped his chest over me yet — '

'That makes you a pretty smart guy,' Maggie Yarmon complimented. 'Did you ever try doing tricks?'

'I've just thought of a good one,' Petersen said without looking at her. 'What happened to the lady with the big mouth.'

'Of all the goddamn nerve . . . '

'Knock it off,' Wayne pleaded. 'Maggie, you ought to get back to the office. Folks'll think we've gone out of business or something.'

Maggie looked at her watch. 'From where I'm standing it's as close to quitting time as makes no difference. But don't worry, Joey, I can take a hint. I'm going. And don't blame me if I have to ride to the jailhouse in the morning to collect the office key.'

She gathered up her hat and handbag and gave Petersen a hard stare before going to the door of the apartment.

'Be seeing you.'

'I'm looking forward to it,' Petersen told her. He winced when the door banged. He lit the cigarette he had taken from Wayne's pack. 'Let's get down to it now, Joe,' he urged. 'The whole works from the word go.'

'Why not?' Wayne touched his head where it hurt. 'At nine this morning I had a call from a dame — '

'At your office? And the dame was Mitzi Laverick?'

'Right both times. She sounded worried. No — frightened would be a better word.'

'But she didn't say she was frightened?'

'Not over the phone she didn't. She made an appointment. She wanted it made as soon as possible. I had just wrapped up a case, so I agreed. I told her to come to my place any time it suited her. She said she would arrive in thirty minutes. She arrived in twenty-five minutes.

'She told me what she wanted with me straight off. She was going to Ashbury today and needed a male escort. She offered me a hundred bucks if I would oblige.'

'That was a lot of money for a small chore,' Petersen broke in. 'Weren't you suspicious at all?'

'I'm always suspicious, Hank. I'm a naturally suspicious guy. I'm also a guy who likes to eat regularly, and the dame's hundred bucks was nothing to sneeze at.'

A movement of the detective's eyebrow told him he agreed.

'You asked her why she needed an escort for a fifty-miles jaunt? Didn't it occur to you that she might be in trouble with the police, and was looking for a blanket to hide under?'

'It did, sure. I asked her what sort of rap she was running away from. She told me it was strictly personal. She said if I didn't believe her I could get in touch with the police.'

'What then?'

'Then I asked her what she was running away from. She told me to mind my own business. She said if I wouldn't stand in for what she wanted, she would get somebody else who would.'

'You let it drop there?'

'Of course I didn't. I've had too many bites from too many dames. I let her know that I operated in accordance with certain codes of conduct. I told her I wasn't exactly popular with the law. I said I was cramming to make the grade for a 'We Love You' card from the cops next Christmas.'

'What happened then?' Petersen asked bleakly.

'She broke down and cried. Yeah, she did. I had to get Maggie Yarmon to lend her some tissues to wipe her nose. Then she admitted that she was scared. I tried to impress on her that being scared is nothing to be ashamed of.'

'How did she take that?' Petersen asked sceptically. He looked at his watch and thought of Floyd Eckert. By now the lieutenant would have drawn anything worth drawing out of the staff at Pace's Pie Parlour. He might be ringing on Wayne's doorbell at any minute.

'Am I boring you?' Wayne asked him.

'All you're doing is giving me a pain, Joe. You know something? I got your number from Pace's Pie Parlour. When I left, Lieutenant Eckert was going over my tracks. You can expect him soon.'

'What's wrong with Eckert? What's wrong with you, Hank? I haven't done a thing I shouldn't have done. I'm in the clear, and nobody can say that I'm not.'

'That makes me breathe easier. Okay, so keep the big confession for Eckert.'

Petersen got up and turned to the apartment door. Wayne stared at his narrow shoulders.

'You want to visit the bathroom?'

Petersen looked back at him when he reached the door.

'It sounds bad enough to me. You used to be able to read your own sign. Not any more you can't, Joe. If you could, you shouldn't be wearing pants. They ought to be scared off you. I know mine would.' Petersen's eyes were cold. He continued. 'Do I have to spell it out in four-letter words? It's what I feel like doing. That was a real nice dame. She didn't look nice when we found her. Her car was tampered with. I ain't so bright, but you don't have to be that bright to read murder. Murder, Joe! Bloody murder. A nice dame is killed in a car. You were driving with her in the car. You jump out, or get thrown out. That makes you smart enough in one sense. But what do you do after that?'

'What did I do?' Wayne asked with brittle humour.

'You figured your neck was too precious to be tramped on by a lot of bulls. You take a powder. You try to forget the whole thing. You bring that goofball dame from the office to hold your nerve together. Forget it, Joe. I'm in no hurry. After Eckert has a talk with you I'll be back. I might be here in an hour's time. I might wait till the middle of the night. I'm not particular when it comes to murder. So-long, Joe.'

Petersen almost walked into Lieutenant Floyd Eckert on the way out. Eckert peered past him to get a glimpse of Wayne.

'Did you soften him up?'

'I thought it was my case, Lieutenant?'

'Nobody's saying. All I'm taking is a fatherly interest. You don't object?'

Under the flat challenge Petersen's jaws darkened.

'I haven't finished with him,' he said.

'Did he clam up on you?'

'No, but — ' Petersen broke off in

confusion and glared at Joe Wayne. 'He had a bad headache. He thought I ought to call again later.'

'I had a bad headache,' Wayne told Eckert. 'I asked Sergeant Petersen if he would come back later.'

'Did you try aspirin?'

'Yeah. It didn't help much.'

Eckert moved into the apartment and Petersen followed him slowly. Eckert took a chair and looked around for something to drink.

'There's beer in the kitchen,' Wayne told him.

'Go get it,' Eckert told Petersen. He tugged his hat off and ran a hand across his head. He glanced quizzically at the strip of Band-Aid. 'Hurt yourself?'

'I had a slight mishap.'

'Don't we all at some time or other? How did you have yours, Wayne?'

'Look, what is this, Lieutenant — '

'It's a question,' Eckert returned smoothly. He took the can of beer that Petersen proffered and poured into a glass. 'You can answer it here, or you can do it down at headquarters. Suit yourself.'

'You call that a choice?'

'I was going to get it out of him,' Petersen said hoarsely.

'You were going out of the door, Hank. I want to hear Wayne's version and I want to hear it now.'

Wayne took a slow breath. His head was paining him again, but if he said so he would get nothing but a sneer from Eckert.

'You're talking about the car smash, Lieutenant.'

'That's right. I've established that you wandered into a café a short distance from the scene a short time after the — uh — accident must have occurred.'

'But it was no accident . . . '

'Now we learn something. See how easy it is, Hank. There's something to be said for the mailed fist after all. Go on, Wayne. It was no accident — Tell me how you worked it out.'

Wayne swallowed his irritation. Petersen had taken another chair and was dividing his attention between him and the lieutenant. His brow was drawn in a worried frown.

'You might not believe it, Lieutenant . . . '

'Five'll get you ten. But you're nothing if not a trier, Joe. Make it snappy too, if you can. We haven't got any time to waste.'

Wayne began all over again. He told the lieutenant about the call to his office from a girl, about the visit from the girl about half an hour later. Her name was Mitzi Laverick. She wished him to accompany her to Ashbury in her car. Wayne had established that she was scared. She wouldn't say what or whom she was scared of. Wayne agreed to take her to Ashbury. She said she would be at his office at a quarter to three.

'I asked her why we couldn't start right away,' he went on. 'She said she needed a few hours to straighen things out.'

'What time did you first hear from her?' Eckert asked.

'Nine this morning. She visited half an hour later.'

'So she turned up in her car at two forty-five. What then?'

'We set off for the Ashbury road — '

'Who was driving?'

'She was driving. On the way I tried to get her to tell me something more about herself. I was curious, you must understand . . . '

'I wondered if you were,' Eckert said drily. 'What did you dig out of her?'

'Nothing.'

'What did you figure?'

'I figured she was leaving somebody in the lurch maybe, perhaps a boy-friend. Not a husband. She wasn't wearing a wedding ring. Like I told Hank, she challenged me to contact the police if I thought she had a record.'

'You didn't?'

'Give me a break, Lieutenant. I believed her.'

'Go on,' Eckert told him curtly. He glanced at Petersen.

'There isn't much left to tell. The last thing I recalled was going into that bend with the fence round it. When I opened my eyes I was still in the car, but the car had gone through the fence. The dame was dead. I had nothing for a memory of events up to then but a big blank.'

'You're kidding!' Eckert looked at Petersen again. Petersen's face was expressionless.

'I'm telling you the truth,' Wayne said coldly. 'I stumbled around for a few minutes, trying to work it all out. I wondered who the dame was, what I was doing there with her. I made sure she was dead. I had a look in her purse and found her name. It didn't mean a thing. Then I noticed that a door was off, that a front wheel was missing. I thought it very odd, so I looked at the hub. The studs that should have held the wheel in place had been filed.

'After a while I went onto the road and started walking. I saw this café and went in to ring for Maggie — '

'Why didn't you ring cops straightaway?'

'Give me time, Lieutenant. I wanted to hear what it was about. I wanted Maggie to pick me up and fill in the details. When she arrived with my car I passed out on her. I was just getting my wind back when Hank called . . . '

'Your memory too, I take it?' Eckert

said suspiciously.

'Is that supposed to be a joke, Lieutenant?'

'It's a question, Wayne. I'm not too keen on this. Are you sure you've told us everything you know?'

'If I think of anything else I'll pass it along.'

Eckert left shortly after that. Petersen lingered for a few more seconds.

'You've just lost a client,' he reminded Wayne. 'I might be back, Joe.'

'You'll always be welcome.'

When the door of the apartment closed once more Wayne brought out the card he had taken from the dead girl's handbag. He had held on to it on impulse. He had refrained from mentioning it on impulse.

He put it into his wallet and went to hunt another drink.

4

Next morning Joe Wayne had the feeling that he was being followed from his apartment on Vine across town to his office in the Wilton Buildings.

When he searched for evidence to substantiate the sensation he could see nothing remotely suspicious looking. Cars were in his wake, of course, but cars were meeting him too, for that matter. As were trucks, station wagons. A couple of planes were even flying overhead.

It was his conscience, he told himself. Only why should he feel guilty about anything? He hadn't filed the studs on the Dodge; he hadn't asked Mitzi Laverick to go riding to Ashbury with him.

If only Mitzi had told him a little more of her business, of the fear that was pressuring her to go in for a change of scene in a hurry.

Last night he had talked the whole thing over with Ruth Foran. Ruth was

Wayne's steady girl-friend. She was an artist and lived out on the suburbs. She and Wayne shared a lot in common, including, perhaps, the belief that one day they would get around to buying a marriage licence. For the present their close relationship was enough for them. Ruth took her innermost worries and problems to Wayne, and he in turn was glad to have a sympathetic ear and a shoulder to lean on when the occasion demanded.

Ruth had been all for his making a clean breast to the police and washing his hands of the Mitzi Laverick affair. According to Ruth, Mitzi Laverick had been the type of girl who made a habit of calling on outside help. Which went without saying that Mitzi had been moving in circles that could turn dangerous at the drop of a hat.

When Wayne asked Ruth to elaborate she pointed to the card he had taken from the girl's purse. Ruth was willing to bet that Mitzi and Morton Cotter had been having fun, and that Cotter's wife, or perhaps one of his girl-friends, had turned jealous and murderous in the one breath, and settled Mitzi Laverick's hash for keeps.

'But that's just a crazy guess,' Wayne had objected. 'The calling card mightn't mean a thing. There could be a hundred and one reasons for the girl having herself killed like that.'

'So okay,' Ruth Foran said calmly. 'But I'm offering you the odd one out. And my advice is to give the card to the cops and tell them where you found it.'

Sound advice, Wayne reflected now as he drew up at a newsstand and bought copies of the *Herald* and the *Chronicle*. Heading back to the car he looked along the road behind him. A car had drawn up at the kerb a dozen yards away. The driver appeared to be a youngish looking blond-haired male. Wayne watched him in his mirror for a few seconds. The view was poor, and after a moment the man left his car and went to the front of a cafeteria.

Wayne sighed and shook out the *Chronicle*. There the story was, on the front page.

Wayne read avidly, looking for mention of his own name. His name wasn't even mentioned. He heaved another sigh, this one of relief, and threw the paper on the seat beside him.

So the girl had been a club singer, he thought as he drove on to the Wilton Buildings. It could tie in with the calling card in his wallet right enough. Maybe he should ride on to Cressley Street and police headquarters and make a contribution of the card he had taken from the girl's handbag.

He remembered that his own name and address had been in the girl's purse as well. Did the two items have a common denominator?

He decided he needed more time to think about it. If he did give the card to the cops eventually and they asked why he had held back, he could always say that recollection had dimmed with his memory lapse and had just returned.

Maggie Yarmon was dealing with the mail when he parked the Plymouth and rode the elevator to his office. She gave him a hard and searing appraisal before poking a cigarette to her mouth and going on with sorting the mail.

'Anything of interest?'

Maggie behaved as though she hadn't heard him. She frowned at a bill and flung it to one side of the desk.

'Have you read the papers yet?'

Maggie took a slow drag on her cigarette and appeared to notice him for the first time.

'What are you doing here?'

'What do you mean, what am I doing here? I work here, as far as I know. Now don't tell me you're going to pull a lost-memory gag just to get your own back on me.'

'Perish the juvenile thought! Lost memory acts are for kids and amateurs. I'm surprised you had the brass nerve to try and pull such a thing on Hank Petersen. That Lieutenant Eckert is suited to anything that anybody pulls on him, though.'

Wayne stared at her.

'Get a load of this! Now we've been

practising telepathy. You left my place yesterday before Eckert arrived. You didn't come back to hold your ear to the door, Maggie?'

Maggie coloured slightly at her mistake; she tried to shrug it off.

'Eckert — Smeckert. I happened to see the guy arriving when I reached the street. And for what it's worth, Joey, I kept my fingers crossed for you the whole of the way home.'

'You figured I was a candidate for a ball and chain. Well, you see how you turned out wrong, and — '

The phone ringing made Wayne break off. He beat Maggie to the receiver.

'Yeah! Joe Wayne here . . . '

'This is me, Joe,' Hank Petersen said. 'I thought I'd give you a buzz after you'd had a good night's sleep.'

'What's having a good night's sleep got to do with anything?' Wayne said suspiciously. He evaded Maggie Yarmon's glittering gaze.

'Well, you said something yesterday about losing your memory. Did you get it patched up?'

'It feels fine at the minute, Hank.'

'Swell. Have you read the papers?'

'Just glanced at them.'

'We played you down, Joe. I guessed you noticed. Too much of the wrong sort of publicity wouldn't do your business a lot of good, huh? Well, I mean, a private detective that has his client practically murdered on his lap . . . You see what I'm driving at, Joe?'

'I'm beginning to get a faint idea,' Wayne said coldly. 'But the stories are played down because I've got friends who are newspapermen, Hank. Not because of any benevolent influence you may have distributed. Also, nobody in his sane senses would imagine I had anything to do with the killing.'

'Like to bet on it?' Petersen growled. 'I'm getting it rough, Joe. Heads are going to rattle if a strong lead isn't soon found and developed. The real reason I called is to ask if you can think of anything — anything, Joe — that you neglected or overlooked passing on.'

Wayne's hesitation while he thought about the calling card was brief.

'I'm sorry, Hank.'

'I counted to five while you paused,' Petersen said curtly. 'You were first on the scene. You could have seen something we didn't see. You could have been told something by the dame that we haven't heard.'

'I wish I could help,' Wayne told him. 'I can't.'

'I see. Where do you go from here?'

'Client-wise, you mean, Hank?'

'How else?' Petersen said with great patience.

'Sit around and wait for something to turn up, I guess. Something usually does, if you sit around for long enough.'

Petersen's reply was inaudible. Wayne suspected the detective was disappointed at his reactions.

'Look, Joe . . . '

'Yeah?'

'There's a possibility — just a possibility — of some sort of repercussion reaching you. Do you follow me?'

'I think so.'

'If it happens you would pass it on to me?'

Wayne laughed shortly.

'What a notion! But okay, Hank. We're old friends from 'way back. You do me a favour; I do you a favour.'

'Thanks, Joe. Thanks a million. So-long for now — '

'Hold it, Hank. You haven't managed to get a lead at all on the dame?'

'We're working hard at it. On her background at the minute. But you know what some of these nightclub canaries can get up to in their mean moments.'

'I can guess. So-long, Hank.'

Wayne hung up and lit a cigarette. He became aware of Maggie staring at him. He lifted his shoulders.

'So okay. So what's with the beady-eyes routine? You don't seriously think I was pulling a gag yesterday, Maggie?'

'What about the visiting card?' Maggie said. 'You just told Hank Petersen you felt fine. That ought to say you can remember the details of the car ride with the dame and what happened afterwards.'

'What did happen afterwards?' Wayne growled suspiciously. 'And what visiting card — I get it! You nasty little so and so, you were meddling in my wallet when I was out for the count. Don't deny it! I can see you're guilty from a mile off.'

'Keep your beard in one piece,' Maggie said scornfully. 'I've been around here for long enough to pick up some tricks of the trade. What kind of secretary would I be anyhow, if I didn't go through your pockets once in a while?'

'Okay, sweet dreams, so you found a calling card in my wallet that I took from Mitzi Laverick's purse. So what? Do you want to make a production out of it? I don't want to rush any fences before I come to them. I want to keep one ace at least up my sleeve. Do you mind very much?'

'The way you shoot the clichés, Joey, a guy would really think you'd lost your brains somewhere,' Maggie said derisively. 'You got a hundred bucks for your trouble, so why can't you get the dame out of your mind?'

'I can't get her out of my mind.'

'But you weren't responsible for her death like that. Grow up, Joe. And there's one interesting sidelight of the affair that appears to have skipped you by.'

'Bring me up to date,' Wayne encouraged. He poked through the mail, studying the latest free samples that Maggie had sent for. There was nothing he could make use of.

'You were in the car when it crashed. Or have you forgotten that too?'

'I might have been found lying there with my toes turned up as well as the dame. Is that what you're driving at, Maggie?'

'It's a hell of a thought to go to bed on,' was the dry rejoinder. 'I know I could get enough material for nightmares from it to last me a month. But why hold something away from the cops? The cops are good guys. The cops have got to live too. What did Hank Petersen ever do to you anyway?'

All good questions, Wayne reflected. And when he came right down to rock bottom he couldn't say exactly why he had held on to Mort Cotter's calling card instead of handing it to Hank Petersen or Eckert yesterday.

'If you don't have a client you don't

have a case,' Maggie explained patiently. 'And I can't see you putting the homicide boys out of business even if you do grow a yen to work for a client that's dead.'

'You think that Cotter could be mixed up in it?'

'I think there is a strong chance he was mixed up in it,' was Maggie's decision. Her gaze narrowed momentarily on Wayne. 'You wouldn't be tempted to go in for a little blackmail on the side, Joey?'

Wayne didn't join in her gusty laugh. He reflected seriously for another two minutes.

'Figure it this way,' he said presently. 'Why would Mitzi have had a card belonging to Morton Cotter?'

'Why didn't you have two heads instead of one?' Maggie said with a snort. 'Around now you could have brought on the spare one. Why would anybody have anybody's calling card?'

'Because he paid a call,' Wayne suggested. 'Take it easy,' he added quickly when Maggie Yarmon drew a breath. 'So if somebody visits and hands you one of his cards it means he wants you to repay the compliment. It means, furthermore, that the said visitor is a comparative stranger to you — '

'And interested in you,' Maggie managed to chip in. 'You know, Joey, you amaze me sometimes. I do believe you've got a strong point there. What you're saying is that Mitzi Laverick and Morton Cotter couldn't have been on intimate terms at all. Which renders the card to the level of waste paper as far as useful evidence goes.'

'Possibly, baby. On the other hand, we must keep an open mind with regards to it.'

'Why must we keep anything open with regards to it, buster? You can't operate for a client that's in the morgue.'

Wayne said sure. He felt very low about the whole business. Mitzi Laverick's life had been in danger. She had entrusted herself to his care from the minute he climbed into her car with her. But how was he to know that the car had been tampered with, and was nothing better than a death wagon?

An hour later there was a call from

Dave Chalmers of the *Herald*. Chalmers knew the full story of the crash on the Ashbury road yesterday.

'I didn't think you'd go for star billing, Joe. The cops said you'd had a memory lapse. That sounded like hundred per cent corn. But you might have been a victim yourself.'

'I know, Dave.'

'Any ideas?' Chalmers asked shrewdly.

'Not a thing. I'm trying to live with it.'

'She was a swell singer, they tell me.'

'You don't have to rub it in, Dave. I didn't fix the wheel so the car would crash.'

'Somebody hated her guts, Joe.'

'I hope the cops find him.'

'You're not very original this morning, are you?' Chalmers complained. 'I was hoping for a scoop.'

'I just want to forget it.'

'Like to take a bet?' Chalmers persisted.

Wayne was about to laugh when something held him back. A tingling sensation raced over his spine.

'I'm not following you, Dave.'

'I didn't think you were. Who are you trying to kid anyhow, Joe? Did the dame divulge anything to you?'

'Not a word.'

'I might believe that, Joe. The cops might even believe it. But how's about the killer?'

'I see!' Wayne said after a moment. 'Now you've really made my day, Dave.'

'It just occurred to me,' Chalmers explained. 'If the dame was worth killing for what she knew, it's quite possible you could be number two pigeon. I'd buy a couple of glass eyes for the back of my head if I were you, Joe.'

'Who said she was killed for what she knew? She could have been killed for what she did. She could have been killed for what she didn't do . . . '

'That's telling him!' Maggie Yarmon applauded. 'It's a wonder you don't surprise yourself with your brilliance now and then.'

'I'm only making guesses,' Chalmers conceded. 'So you're twiddling your thumbs until a new case comes in?'

'Now I think I'll spend the time making

a will,' Wayne said sourly. 'Goodbye, Dave.'

'Sure!' Chalmers grunted. 'Be good, Joe.'

Wayne replaced the receiver and lit a cigarette. He thought it odd that everybody doubted his word. He thought it odd that everybody suspected he was holding something back. When he glanced at Maggie Yarmon he noticed the same doubts clouding her eyes.

'But what did I do, for pete's sake!'

'Quit worrying,' Maggie told him. She added philosophically, 'You'll die if you worry; you'll die if you don't.'

Wayne didn't answer her. After a minute Maggie shrugged and began beating at her typewriter. Wayne was staring out of the window when the phone rang again. This time Maggie lifted the handpiece and spoke.

'Wayne Investigations! Yeah, that's right. Yeah, he is. Look, Hank, why can't you leave the mutt alone — '

'Give me that.' Wayne grabbed the receiver and snapped into it. 'This is Wayne . . . '

'I've got some news for you.' Petersen sounded weary and irritated. 'This is a lulu.'

'The suspense is killing me, Hank. Cough it up.'

'I've just got a full report of the autopsy on the dead girl, Joe. It's going to break your heart.'

'Knock it off, Hank. I haven't got a heart — remember?'

'Mitzi Laverick was four months pregnant.'

'What!'

'I thought it would throw you, Joe. It's all very sad, ain't it? But it might give us the lead we could use about now . . . '

Wayne only half heard the rest of Petersen's talk. He grunted after a few seconds and put the phone down. He told Maggie the news and watched her cheeks pale. Maggie cursed fluently for a full minute.

'You'll just have to do something, Joey,' she snarled finally. 'I'll never look you straight in the eye again if you don't.'

An impatient ringing of the doorbell put Wayne to crossing the office quickly.

He expected nobody but Lieutenant Floyd Eckert to be on the other side of the door. It wasn't the lieutenant he found himself staring at. It was a young man with blond hair and grey eyes. The same young man he had imagined was following him earlier.

5

'Joseph Wayne?'

'That's right. What can I do for you?'

'I want to talk to you, Mr. Wayne.'

The visitor eased past Wayne until he was inside the office and facing Maggie Yarmon.

'How do you do?' he said then in a polite voice.

'To be quite frank with you, I'm not at my best. Is there some way we can help you?'

'My name is Dell Lavers.' He swung to look at Joe Wayne again. Wayne was closing the office door slowly.

'Dell Lavers? That could mean . . . '

'That I'm related to Mitzi Laverick,' Lavers finished for him. His tone was cool and even. 'I happen to be her brother, in fact.'

Wayne's eyes had narrowed on him, remembering how Lavers or Laverick, or whatever, had been sitting on his tail this morning at the newsstand.

'Can you prove that?'

Lavers coloured a little. 'Prove what, Mr. Wayne — that my name is Dell Lavers?'

'That Mitzi Laverick was your sister,' Wayne said.

'Of course she was my sister. The family name is Lavers. When Mitzi wanted to become a professional entertainer Dad objected. My father had very straitlaced views on some things, Mr. Wayne — '

'Had?'

'Yes. He died a year ago. We were a New York family originally. Mitzi took off six months ago and came west. I heard she'd been making quite a name for herself. I had a job in New York, but I wanted to travel west myself. Before Dad died he asked me to find Mitzi and keep an eye on her.'

Wayne looked at him for a moment. Maggie Yarmon was coughing loudly to catch Wayne's attention. He saw she was performing some kind of mime, like examining an object in her hand.

'So you didn't find your sister?' Wayne said. 'Would you like to sit down while we chat? You can come on into my private office if you wish,' he added.

'Joe's afraid of me hearing too many secrets,' Maggie explained to Lavers with a frosty smile. 'When I find anything useful I usually sell it to one of our competitors.'

Lavers's hesitation was brief.

'Well, I was thinking of going into some detail — '

'The sealed room it is, my lad,' Maggie encouraged. She put a cigarette to her lips and asked the blond for a light. When Lavers leaned forward to oblige Maggie ogled him. 'My, but you are a good-looking guy. Didn't anybody ever tell you how handsome you are?'

'You're just kidding, Miss — '

'Yarmon. Maggie Yarmon. Everybody introduces himself around here. You don't mind? And in case I forget to tell you before you leave, I could be free for a dinner date this evening.'

Lavers laughed shortly and looked at Wayne for help.

Wayne had a pained expression on his face and gestured to the inner door. Lavers nodded to Maggie and walked quickly towards it. Wayne stared at her before following the caller.

'What are you setting up?' he hissed.

'Be your age, Joey. All I'm doing is showing him how pally we really are. By the look in his eye he's going to slay somebody over his sister before lunch.'

In his office Wayne closed the door and waved the newcomer to a chair. He went behind his desk and ducked to bring a bottle to light.

'Drinks?'

'No thanks, Mr. Wayne. I just want to talk.'

Wayne shrugged and smiled faintly. He interlocked his fingers on top of the desk.

'You say you're Dell Lavers. You could be Dell Lavers for all I know, but — '

'Here's my driving licence.' Lavers produced it and Wayne checked with it.

'So far so good. You also said you are a brother of Mitzi Laverick . . . '

'What would I be doing here if I wasn't?' Lavers reasoned.

'Sure! But if you had some way of proving that too it would clear the air to some extent.'

'I've got a letter she wrote to me.' Lavers searched in his pocket and produced an envelope. He paused with it half way extended to Wayne. 'But you might say I forged it for some reason or other.'

'Let's see it anyhow.'

Wayne opened the envelope and drew out the letter. He glanced through it briefly. It had been written some months before and told Lavers that the writer was fine and well, and was thoroughly enjoying herself. It was signed simply, 'Mitzi'.

Wayne produced his wallet and took from it the slip of paper he had found in Mitzi Laverick's handbag. It was obvious that the person who had made a note of his address on the slip of paper, and the person who had penned the letter to Lavers, were one and the same. He pushed the letter into its envelope and tossed the envelope back to Dell Lavers.

'I'm sorry about what happened to

your sister, Dell. I take it you're calling on me on account of the car crash?'

Lavers drew a deep breath and nodded. A grimness had entered the grey eyes and grooved lines at the corners of his mouth.

'I want to hear what happened, Mr. Wayne. Everything.'

'Yeah. I guess you do, Dell. Have you been to the police, by the way?'

'I have,' he said flatly.

'What did they tell you?'

'They told me my sister hired you to accompany her to another town. They said the car you travelled in had been tampered with. The car crashed and my sister was killed.'

'That's just about it in a nutshell,' Wayne agreed.

'Why did my sister hire you?' Lavers asked him.

'She said she was scared. She rang me up yesterday morning and made an appointment. She told me what she wanted me to do for her. She offered me a hundred dollars to accompany her to Ashbury in her car. I took it that I was to act as some kind of bodyguard. I tried to get your sister to talk about it. She wouldn't.'

'Did you believe her?'

Wayne's eyebrows rose. 'How do you mean, did I believe her?'

'That she was scared. Did she act scared? Did she sound scared?'

'She did, as a matter of fact. And then some. I tried pumping her, but she wasn't having anything. And then — Well, we must have reached the bad bend by that time. The next thing I knew was opening my eyes in the car with Mitzi Laverick. I couldn't remember right off who she was. I must have suffered some kind of amnesia.

'I wasn't so far gone that I didn't decide to have a look round to see what had happened. I saw the door had been wrenched from the car. I saw the wheel had parted company with the car — '

'The wheel had been deliberately fixed so that it would come off on the first bend,' Lavers interrupted.

'That's it, Dell. It looked like your sister had outgrown her usefulness to somebody.' Wayne paused there to see if

Lavers would fill in with what Petersen had said over the phone. He didn't. Wayne rubbed his jaw. There was something clean-cut and wholesome about the blond man that triggered off a sympathy with him. 'Didn't the cops tell you anything else about your sister?'

Lavers frowned. 'What are you talking about?'

'I don't know whether I ought to tell you, Dell. But I don't suppose it matters if I do — '

'For the love of mike spill it,' the other snapped hoarsely. 'Do they have a clue as to who tampered with the car?'

'If they have I don't know about it. I do know that Mitzi was four months pregnant.'

Had he hit Lavers between the eyes the effect could hardly have been more startling. The blond surged to his feet and struck Wayne's desk a hammer blow with his fist. The grey gaze was afire just then.

'It's a dirty lie!' he snarled savagely. 'You're just saying that because . . . '

'Because of what?' Wayne said coolly when his words tailed away. 'Why should

I repeat anything of the sort if I didn't get it for the truth?'

'Oh, no!'

Lavers covered his face with his hands and sagged onto his chair again. Wayne gave him a few moments to compose himself. When he withdrew his hands his cheeks were suddenly drawn and haggard.

'Who — who told you this?'

'The cops. A short time ago. I'm friendly with the sergeant who's covering the case.'

'He must be found!' Lavers mouthed harshly. 'Don't you see, Mr. Wayne, he must be found . . . '

'He will be found, Dell,' Wayne consoled him. 'The cops have ways and means.'

'The police!' Lavers snorted derisively. 'What do you think brought me to see you anyway?'

'To hear how I was with your sister when the car she was driving crashed. Had you anything else on your mind?'

Lavers's fingers trembled as he brought a cigarette to his lips and lit it. He puffed steadily for ten seconds, never taking his eyes from Wayne's.

'I intended putting a proposition to you, Mr. Wayne,' he said then.

'Like getting me to stand still until you managed to tie a can to my tail?' Wayne hazarded.

Lavers's jaws tinged with colour again. 'I admit I followed you from your home. I couldn't quite make up my mind to approach you and get your reactions.'

'To what, Dell?' Wayne asked interestedly.

Lavers made another pause. He seemed to come to a decision. 'I was going to ask you to hunt for the man who wanted my sister out of the way. Now I'm more determined than ever to have the murderer — he's nothing less than a murderer — caught and brought to justice.'

Wayne's laugh was threadbare.

'Take it easy, Dell. I can understand how you're worked up about this — '

'I'm not worked up,' he objected. 'I'm as calm and collected as you are. I know the angles.'

'Do you know the police?'

The blond man's lips twisted. 'I've talked with them. Oh, they offered me plenty of sympathy, sure. Sympathy is one of the cheapest commodities going. But back of it all I could see what they were thinking — '

'You could be wrong, Dell.'

'I'm not wrong, Mr. Wayne. I know the score. My sister had the name of being a night-club singer. Night-club canaries come at a dollar a dozen. Now if Mitzi had been the wife or sister of one of the top-ranking citizens in town . . . '

'You really are away off,' Wayne broke in again. 'I know the local police force, Dell. Especially do I know the guy that's been put in charge of this case.'

'A sergeant!'

'He's a very good sergeant. I know how he works. I get along with him. If he's got a tip that I need he passes it along. I do the same if I can help him.'

'You call that a recommendation?'

'I'm just telling you that your sister's case will get the same treatment from the homicide boys as anybody's case would get.'

'I'd like to believe you, Mr. Wayne.'

'You can believe me, Dell.'

Lavers puffed quietly for a moment. Then, 'She's been playing around with some bastard. He didn't want to marry her. Or he was in no position to marry anybody. If only I knew who he is!'

'The cops will find out.'

Lavers sighed and rose to his feet. He was heading for the door when he halted and came back to hold out his hand.

'Thanks anyhow, Wayne.'

'For what? I feel as bitter as you do. I feel as inadequate as you do. It's going to be quite a while before I can get to sleep at night.'

'And you're a busy man, I take it?'

'When I'm busy I'm a very busy man,' Wayne agreed.

'But you took my sister's assignment.'

'I did, of course. A hundred dollars for a drive in the country.'

'But you guessed there could be danger involved?'

Wayne wondered what he was probing for. He inclined his head slowly.

'I knew your sister was hot and

bothered. I figured that maybe she was running away from a too passionate love affair, or something of the sort.'

'That's for sure,' Lavers grated. His brow clouded. 'Look, Mr. Wayne, I'm going to ask you right out — will you help me?'

'Help you? How, Dell?'

'Find this guy for me.'

'But the police — '

'The hell with the police! They'll go through the motions. But the very nature of the tactics they'll adopt will make it easy for the killer of Mitzi to slip out of their fingers. I'm not asking you to do this out of charity, Wayne. I've got a good job. I can pay you. You admit it'll be a long time before you can forget what happened. You could have been killed as easily as Mitzi, when you think about it.'

Wayne grinned faintly. 'I have thought about it. Plenty.' He mulled the thing over while Lavers waited hopefully.

'Please, Mr. Wayne! I hear you've got a good reputation in this town.'

'Okay, Dell. I'll not give you any promises at the minute. What I will do is think about it. I'll have to get the all clear from the cops, of course. Murder is hardly my line. There are lots of other problems waiting to be solved.'

'When can you give me your decision?' Lavers asked eagerly. 'I'm stopping at an apartment house over on the east side. I'll stick by the phone until I hear from you. If you like, I can hang around here until you say the word.'

'That won't be necessary. Give me your address and your phone number.'

Lavers took a ballpen from his pocket and scribbled on a piece of paper. He extended his hand once more.

'I'm hoping against hope you'll operate for me, Mr. Wayne.'

'I'll think about it, Dell. Can you find your own way to the door?'

When Lavers had left Wayne continued to sit on his chair and smoke. After a few minutes the intercom on the desk buzzed.

'I'm getting hellish anxious about you, Joe. Did he hit you under the belt?'

'Yeah, he did. Now why don't you just get on with your knitting, honey?'

'Okay, buster. If that's the way you

want it. There's enough deep freeze around this joint to encourage a dame to declare herself redundant.'

'I'm sorry, Maggie. I'm thinking.'

'That ought to be very nice for you, Joey. I never knew you to brag about it.'

Wayne reached for the phone presently and dialled police headquarters. He contacted Communications and asked if Hank Petersen was around.

'Sergeant Petersen is out. Will somebody else do?'

'How about Lieutenant Eckert?'

Eckert spoke to him when a minute had ridden by. He announced himself and said, 'How can I help?'

'This is Joe Wayne, Lieutenant. I've got a kind of deal I'd like to make with you.'

Eckert snorted into the mouthpiece.

'Okay. I've got my blood pressure under control. What is it, Wayne?'

'Mitzi Laverick's brother has been here. He wants me to take an interest in the whereabouts of the killer. I could snoop around without telling you, of course, Lieutenant, but — '

'You just know better, Joe, don't you?

Look, do you have any leads that you didn't tell us about?'

'Not a clue. I'd be starting off from scratch. And after all, Lieutenant, I could have been found dead in that smash as well as the dame.'

'You do say! How did her brother strike you, Joe?'

'He seems a nice guy. He doesn't have anything against the police. He's just anxious to have the killer caught as soon as possible.'

Silence at the other end for a minute. A garble of voices came through, then, 'All right, Joe. So long as you keep in touch. So long as you don't give us any runaround. And remember, you'll be needed at the coroner's inquest. He doesn't see any reason for holding it up. Eleven o'clock down here in the morning?'

'I'll be there, Lieutenant. Thanks for everything.'

'Yeah!' Eckert said and hung up.

Wayne went out to Maggie and told her what was in the wind.

'It's the first decent thing you've done

in days, Joey,' was her pleased response. 'So where do you want to leap off from?'

'The clippings file,' Wayne said. 'Get busy on it, Maggie. See what you can dig up on Mort Cotter. Then see what you can dig up on Mitzi Laverick. You're bound to have friends that visit the sort of club Mitzi worked at.'

'That's what I like about you,' Maggie flung back. 'You let on to be the big brain around here. But, I ask you, who does the real drudgery? And don't forget the kind of spot you're going to be on if this crazy killer thinks you're getting too close to the bone.'

It was the killer that Wayne was thinking about just then.

6

It was noon next day when the coroner's inquest was wound up. The chief witnesses were Joe Wayne, the motorcycle cop, Lashlin, who had discovered the wrecked car, and the dead girl's brother, Dell Lavers.

Wayne had already told Lavers that he would take his case. The blond man had called at the office in the Wilton Buildings twenty minutes afterwards, to shake Wayne's hand again and give him a retainer cheque for five hundred dollars.

As they headed out of the City Hall quarters Wayne by-passed Lavers who wanted to talk with him and caught the motorcycle cop when he hit the street.

'Excuse me!'

Lashlin wheeled and eyed Wayne warily as he came up. He had stuck a piece of gum in his mouth and rolled it around.

'What is it, Mr. Wayne? I'm supposed to get right back on duty.'

Wayne grinned. 'Without even a cup of coffee?'

'Lookit, you might have an interest in this thing. I said nothing back there only what I saw.'

'So you can't take time off for a cup of coffee? I tell you what — it's nearly lunchtime anyhow — Let me treat you to a steak, potatoes and apple pie.'

Lashlin considered private detectives as a breed entirely apart from his own calling. He saw them with jaundiced eyes and in an aura of distasteful connotations. He knew however that Joe Wayne had obtained permission to make his own investigations. He decided that Wayne must have some saving graces which had escaped him. He relented under Wayne's smile.

'If you hadn't thrown in the apple pie you'd have to eat on your own. And what's wrong with being treated?'

'You tell me.'

They ate at a small restaurant not far from the building they had just left. Over coffee Wayne focused on his reason for wanting to talk with Lashlin.

'You didn't see anybody around the scene at all, Tom?'

Lashlin chuckled. 'Like the guy who filed the studs off the wheel hub? That would be making it real easy for you, Joe, wouldn't it? No, I didn't see a thing. It was the fence that caught my eye, like I said. I went over the rocks for a better look and there she was . . . '

'Sad.'

'Sad as hell. She was some looker too. I wish I had the punk who did it by the short hairs. I'd make him sing a tune all right.'

'Me too,' Wayne said. 'Times of day there isn't a lot of traffic on that road. Some folks travelling to Ashbury would rather use the highway and the Ashbury fork. It's a longer way round, but you get there all the same.'

Lashlin drained his coffee and took the cigarette that Wayne proffered. His heavy-lidded eyes narrowed in puzzlement.

'What are you really driving at? I didn't have a memory lapse like you had. All I had was bees in my stomach when I saw the dame.'

Wayne shrugged. 'Nothing, I guess. Just a hunch that you might have spoken to somebody, that you might have seen somebody and it slipped your mind.'

Lashlin thought for a moment. He popped gum into his mouth.

'There was just this guy that slowed when I came back to my machine. A rubber-neck. I told him to buzz off.'

'He didn't stop?'

'I didn't want him to stop. In no time there would have been a bottle-neck and another car crash maybe.'

'So you didn't get a gander at the rubber-neck, Tom?'

Lashlin frowned at him. 'You don't think . . . But no. If the guy had been in on it he would have been twenty miles away by then.'

'Sure he would. I — '

'Hey, hold on!' the cop breathed.

'Has something got a grip on your leg?'

'When you come to mention it, Joe, there was something about that guy was familiar. I mean I'm sure I saw him around somewhere before.'

Wayne didn't show any eagerness. He smiled faintly.

'Somebody you gave a ticket to,' he suggested.

Lashlin picked at his teeth with a match while he thought about it. 'Who else could he be? I've seen him around town. Don't know his name though. But you're only looking for a fall guy. I know the way you feel, Joe. There's no law against looking.'

'Guess not. What did he come over like — fat, thin? Tall, short?'

'Hard to say. Plenty sun-tanned, if you see what I mean. Black eyes. He was driving a grey Ford. Forget it. The jerk we want will be lying low some place.'

'I bet he is. Another cup of coffee?'

Lashlin shook his head. He said he would have to be going and stood up.

'Thanks for the chuck, Mr. Wayne. Maybe I'll do you a favour some time.'

Maybe he already had, Wayne thought when he parted with the cop on the street. Whoever had fixed the wheel of Mitzi Laverick's car might have followed it when it left his office. A dark-faced man with black eyes. The description didn't fit anyone that Wayne knew. It was something to file away for future reference, he decided.

He got into his car and cruised out to the north end of town. The sky was clear and the heat was beating down on everything. He reached Columbus Avenue and slowed on the approach to *Greenmere*, which was the name of the house where Morton Cotter lived.

It wasn't simply a house: *Greenmere* was the closest thing to a castle that Joe Wayne had ever seen. A long asphalt drive wound through flower gardens interspersed with stretches of lush lawn to a large concrete area where half a dozen swank cars were parked. Beside them Wayne's Plymouth looked as out of place as a glass bead in a cluster of rubies.

When he stepped out of the Plymouth he heard birds chirping near by; when he slammed the door of the car the birds ceased chirping and a dog commenced barking.

Wayne was unprepared for a huge Alsatian that bounded at him from the left-hand corner of the house, jaws hanging malevolently, teeth shining in the hot sunlight. He realised that the brute could be trained to rip out the throats of visitors who hadn't taken the precaution of announcing their intentions. He slipped his fingers under his jacket and whipped out the .38 automatic that nestled there.

He was levelling the gun at the bounding dog when a harsh cry vibrated over the scene.

'Don't shoot, you damned fool!'

'Call him off then.'

'Down, Howard! Down, boy. Come here!'

The dog's stride broke in mid-air as though a mallet had been wielded on its big skull. It flopped to the asphalt on all fours and wriggled towards Wayne on its stomach.

'Are you sure that did it?'

'Don't move. Put your gun out of sight. Howard doesn't like guns.'

'I can't say that I altogether go for Howard.'

Wayne returned his gun to its holster

and smoothed down his sports coat. The man who had come forward was small and chunky, with a bald head and long, jutting jawline. The thin moustache on his upper lip struck an incongruous note. He was dressed in rumpled gaberdine slacks and yellow sweatshirt. His bare arms were thick as young tree trunks, liberally coated with a rich golden down.

He had a lengthy leash in his hands and stooped to secure it to the dog's collar. With the free end of the lash he gave the Alsatian a hard cut on the haunch.

'You stay when I tell you. Get it?'

He was breathing unevenly, which told Wayne he might not be the personification of physical fitness that he looked. His bright blue eyes swept the visitor from the shoes up. Then the glance skidded to the dusty Plymouth and the small, rather pudgy mouth quirked noticeably.

'You shouldn't have pulled a gun on Howard,' he rebuked sternly. 'He doesn't like guns.'

'You've already said that. What was I supposed to pull on him to keep him at bay — a funny gag?'

'You don't know how lucky you are. Next time you come here I'd advise you to whistle softly. Howard finds it kind of soothing.'

'I must remember that.'

The bulky man gave the dog another cuff with the end of the leash, then started leading the animal to the side of the house again. He was almost out of sight when Wayne found his tongue.

'This is *Greenmere*, isn't it?'

The man halted to stare at him.

'I figured you knew your way around.'

'I don't, as a matter of fact. I'm calling on Mr. Cotter. Is he in?'

'Does he know?'

'It's in the nature of a pleasant surprise. You don't have to tie a leash on him?'

The man just glared. He didn't say anything. He disappeared and Wayne went on to the four steps leading to the front door. As he reached the steps the door opened and a lean man in well-cut grey suit emerged. He carried a brief-case under one arm and smiled vaguely at Wayne on his way to the parked cars. Wayne waited to see which one he would get into. The thin man chose the Maserati sports job and buzzed on to the drive.

When Wayne turned his head he found himself confronted by a soberly clad and sober-faced butler.

'Goodday, sir.'

'Is Mr. Cotter at home?'

'He's just resting after lunch, sir. He doesn't like to be disturbed when he's resting after lunch. Do you have an appointment with him?'

Wayne grinned meagrely and produced the card he had taken from Mitzi Laverick's handbag. The butler took it gingerly and glanced at it. Then Wayne was aware of a swift and all-embracing scrutiny.

'This is Mr. Cotter's card, sir.'

'Exactly. The proof of the pudding . . .'

'I'd prefer to have your card, sir.'

'I'm so sorry. I gave my last one to a friendly Alsatian I met on the way here. He looked so frightening and I figured it might keep his mind occupied for a minute. I could let you have my autograph, though. Cheap.'

'Your word will be enough to get along

with. And, as I explained to you — '

'I know. Mr. Cotter is relaxing after lunch. Tell Mr. Cotter that Joseph Wayne is calling. If that doesn't fetch him I don't know what will. And the card again, if you please.'

The butler palmed it before he could grab it back. A thin smile did nothing to enhance his features. He opened the door wider and led Wayne into a hall that could have taken six pool tables with a game going on at each of them. Half-way along the deep-piled carpet he halted and pointed to a pseudo-antique chair against the wall.

'If you will wait here.'

'If you don't bring on a pack of wolfhounds.'

Wayne watched his steady and unhurried progress to a bend in the hall where the butler went from view. He sat down on the chair but got up immediately to study some prints hanging above him. They might be prints, he thought. Again, they might be the real thing. He had never met Morton Cotter, but he had heard a lot about him. Cotter was rich enough to pander to any number of artistic whims.

Two minutes had passed and Wayne was lighting a cigarette when the butler came into sight again. The thin smile still lurked on his face and it had a smug, satisfied quality that told Wayne the worst before he opened his mouth.

'I'm so sorry, Mr. Wayne . . . '

'What happened? Hasn't Cotter had all the rest he needs for the moment?'

'He can't see you today, sir.'

'I see.' Wayne puffed at his cigarette despite the disapproving frown that began to build. 'When can I have an audience with him?'

'I'm sorry, sir — '

'I can tell that by the way you're crying your eyes out. Answer my question: when can he see me?'

'Not at all, Mr. Wayne. Mr. Cotter is a very busy man and — Hold on, sir!'

He cried that when Wayne strode past him to the bend in the hall. Wayne came up short when two men in tan slacks and tweed jackets stepped into his path.

They were both slim and wiry looking;

both appeared to be anticipating some rare pleasure in the very near future. The butler bustled up at Wayne's back.

'Of all the brass nerve!' he grated in a trembling voice.

'What's to do with the mug?' the dark man on Wayne's left said from flat lips.

'I want to see Mr. Cotter.'

'He's busy. You can't see him.'

'Why doesn't somebody make up his mind around here? Last report I had Cotter was pandering to his digestive juices. I won't keep him long.'

When he tried to get between the pair a set of active fingers fastened onto his shoulder.

'Why don't you wise up and get the message?' the dark man inquired. 'About face and take off. If you want to speak to the boss you can try reaching him by phone.'

As he spoke he dug his fingers into Wayne's shoulder muscle. At the same time a subtle challenge glinted in his eye.

'Put your hand back where it came from,' Wayne murmured.

'When you make up your mind to play

to our rules, pal,' was the curt response. 'Go, boy, go!'

He gave Wayne a heave that upset him into his companion. His companion poked his knuckles at Wayne's chest.

'Let him alone,' the butler panted. 'I can handle him.'

'Too many cooks . . . ' Wayne reminded him. His balled fist connected with the dark man's jaw and put him into a diving circle that broke when he toppled to his knees. Wayne was spinning to the other tough when the barrel of a gun was jabbed against his ribs.

'Stay right there!'

'Spoil sport,' Wayne jeered.

The dark man came off his knees and threw a looping right. Wayne tried to duck it but was caught on the side of the face. The punch lacked sting. The gun bored at Wayne's ribs. The butler lamented.

'Leave him alone!'

Wayne was struck twice in the face by the dark man while his friend held the gun levelled to shoot if he attempted to retaliate. The butler hurried past and opened a door.

'Please, Mr. Cotter — '

Wayne was absorbing a rain of blows when a curt, incisive cry reached them.

'What the hell is going on? Nate! Rod! Cut out the comedy. Who is this guy?'

'Joe Wayne,' Wayne mumbled. He dragged air to his lungs and pointed at the pair. 'Get replacements while the going's good. You won't have these dummies tomorrow when I meet them on level terms.'

'He wanted to barge in on you,' the dark man explained. 'He wouldn't take no for an answer.'

'That's right, Mr. Cotter,' the butler contributed. 'You said you didn't wish to see him.'

'I didn't say to get rough with anybody. What do you want with me, Wayne?'

'I wanted to talk,' Wayne said. He loosened his tie and touched a bruise on his jawbone that was beginning to hurt.

Morton Cotter was a medium-built man of around forty. He had eyes of a very light blue that tended to bulge somewhat. His hair was fair and beginning to thin out a little at the temples.

The eyes when they touched Wayne's oscillated like restless fireflies.

'What did you want to talk about?'

'You might call it business.'

'What is your business?'

'I'm a private investigator.'

'I might have guessed!' the dark man sneered. 'Let's take care of him properly, Mr. Cotter . . . '

'In a minute,' Cotter said. His tone had no feeling now. He regarded Wayne in the manner he would regard a smut of dirt on his white shirt. 'What possible dealings could you have with me, Wayne?'

'You own some night clubs.'

'I own lots of things. So what?'

'I'll settle for the night-club angle.' Wayne touched his mouth now and looked for blood. There was a faint streak when he brought his hand away.

'You'll settle for nothing, friend,' Cotter retorted coldly. 'Get the devil out of here before you really get something to remember me by. Two things I can't stand, Wayne — morons and snoopers. You're the right combination of both to make me puke.'

'You're a pretty smart guy, Cotter.'

'I'm smart enough. Now do you shove?'

'Okay. Have it as you want it. But maybe you'll be glad to talk to me one of these days. Pretty soon at that.'

'I don't get you,' Cotter snapped tautly.

'You will, pal. In good time. Soon as you remember that a dame called Mitzi Laverick used to work for you.'

It was hard to know if it meant anything to Cotter. Wayne didn't wait till he thought about it. He straightened his coat and walked rapidly to the front door. Nobody said a word to stop him. Nobody made a move to stop him. He didn't breathe easy until he was behind the wheel of the Plymouth.

7

He had to brake sharply when he met a car slewing from the road into the driveway. The black, anonymous vehicle came to a halt in sifting dust and the driver stuck his head out.

'What are you doing here?'

'Hello, Hank,' Wayne greeted Petersen. 'I always suspected we operated on similar wave-lengths.'

'Yeah,' Petersen grunted. He saw the bruises on Wayne's face and his eyes narrowed. 'Where did you get those?'

'From Cotter's glamour boys. He keeps a whole houseful of them, Hank. I'd watch how I go if I were you.'

'Let them try — Say, what are you doing here anyhow?'

'Slumming. I made a big mistake. I — '

'Knock it off. We're on the level with each other or you go out of my scheme of things with a bang.'

Wayne poked a cigarette to his mouth

and rested his elbow on the window frame.

'Simple. I knew that Mitzi worked some clubs in Darton City. I knew that friend Cotter owns some clubs in Darton City. The rest was sheer brain-work.'

'Ahuh!' Petersen knocked his hat up and looked on to the house. 'I wish I could have made it first, Joe. Now he'll think you cried cop.'

'I'll stick around to hear how you make out, Hank. But watch for the Alsatian.'

'Let me at the punk,' Petersen said and gunned his car forward.

Wayne drove onto the road and continued for a quarter mile. He parked and switched on the radio. He got a pop programme and adjusted the volume. Then he looked at his face in the saloon mirror. There wasn't much showing for his tussle with the two athletes. He hoped he would get a chance to give them a proper work-out.

It was fifteen minutes before Hank Petersen's car drifted up to the tail of the Plymouth. Petersen got out and came round to sit beside Wayne. There was nothing on his gaunt features to show what his thoughts were.

'Kind regards from Morton Cotter. Deepest regrets too, Joe. He's very sorry for what happened to you.'

'You're kidding, Hank. Did he say that?'

Petersen lit a cigarette and knocked his hat back. 'Yeah, he did.' He puffed smoke at the roof. 'He said something about you giving the butler a card. The whole thing smelled like a fifth-rate gag to him. He says he's always being pestered — by guys who want him to sponsor their talents in the theatre or TV, but nuts, cranks, what have you — '

'And private eyes?' Wayne said drily.

'He only gets them every other year. What was your general opinion of the guy?'

'I never got a chance to judge, Hank. All I sniffed was that dog's hot breath and the aroma of moolah that pervades the joint. Did you get to base with the two mugs that keep the draughts out?'

Petersen shook his head.

'What put you onto him, Joe?'

'Simple deduction, like I told you, Hank. You arrived here by the same course, I take it.'

'Where did you pick up the calling card?'

'Let me think. I must have found it lying around.'

'Okay.' Petersen opened the door and threw a leg out. 'I'm sorry too, Joe. But we can't co-operate on your terms. They're not the terms we decided on.'

'You can't brush me off, Hank . . . '

'I can brush you off,' Petersen said. He got onto the road and slammed the door. 'So-long, Joe.'

'No. Wait, Hank. I didn't think it was worth mentioning. If you really must know, I found the card in the dame's purse.'

'Mitzi Laverick's?' Petersen's eyes were cold.

'Yeah. I didn't want to brew a storm in a teacup.'

'I call that concealing evidence, pal. You're a big boy. You ought to know better. What else did you find?'

'Nothing. Well, just a slip of paper with

my address on it. There's a perfectly good explanation for that. The dame copied it from the phone book when she called me in the first place.'

'I don't know, Joe. I think you should lay off.'

'Listen, Hank, nobody's pushing me off this case. Nobody. If I hadn't gotten permission I'd have gone ahead anyway. I could be in the morgue now too, you know. Maybe it was me the killer was really after. Did you ever think about the angle?'

Petersen stroked his chin. 'All right,' he said gruffly. 'But we play together or I drop you like a hot potato.'

'Swell,' Wayne grinned. 'Want to shake on it?'

Petersen looked pained and went back to his car. Wayne brought the Plymouth to life and moved off in front of him.

★   ★   ★

Dell Lavers was waiting for him when he reached his office. Lavers had taken the trouble of compiling a list of his sister's known friends and acquaintances. He had also discovered some of the clubs where his sister had worked.

'I hope you don't mind me doing this, Mr. Wayne. But I felt I couldn't sit around just doing nothing to catch this killer, whoever he is.'

A stern retort formed on Wayne's lips, but he caught Maggie's eye and held it back. He took the typed sheets and glanced at them before tossing them to the desk.

'You did all that yourself?'

'I've been busy since I heard the news. I — I wasn't sure that you would operate for me . . . '

'But now you are, Dell,' Wayne said patiently. 'Now you see that I am operating on your behalf. So are the police — '

'And if you don't believe that Joe's doing his best for you, Dell, take a hard look at his kisser. If that doesn't impress you I don't know what will.'

'Of course! Have you been in a fight, Mr. Wayne?'

'A small difference of opinion, Dell.

There's a difference between that and a fight, as you ought to know.'

'Where did you have it, Joey? It bears all the trademarks of an attempt to ravish some — Oh, I'm so sorry, Dell. Such things are not for your gorgeous pink ears.'

Lavers laughed raggedly.

'I wish you wouldn't keep treating me like somebody who has spent his life wrapped up in cotton wool, Miss Yarmon. I'm not as young and callow as I look.'

'I bet you're not, Dell boy. And if I was five years younger myself I'd say we could make a tempestuous twosome — '

Wayne broke in before she could continue.

'Where did you get that stuff typed, Dell?'

'Why, I — I had a girl at the office do it. I didn't do anything wrong, I hope.'

'Just don't do it again is all,' Wayne told him. 'I mean it, Dell. The old saw about two heads being better than one isn't the golden gem it's been drummed up to be. Do you follow me?'

Lavers nodded. He was contrite and apologetic.

'I'll not meddle any more, Mr. Wayne. I'll leave everything in your hands.'

'Do that, Dell. You can slam the door if you like on the way out.'

Maggie Yarmon held her breath until the confused Lavers had left the office. Then she released it gustily.

'Of all the goddam, ill-mannered pinheads — '

'Let it ride, baby. His intentions might be good. The results could only complicate matters. When an amateur dabbles in the professional's field he usually makes nightmares for everybody concerned.'

'Did I call you pinhead, Joey? I'm sorry. From where I'm sitting it's about half the size of this room. Who hit you, anyhow? Where did you go?'

Wayne told her of his visit to *Greenmere* and the reception he had there. Maggie's eyes narrowed thoughtfully.

'That could be your man.'

'I went about it the wrong way, I guess. I should have stayed in cover and sniffed around for a while. Then Hank Petersen turned up. Petersen didn't get much joy either. He's typical cop. Routine investigation. Routine questions. For my money the cops will do nothing but make the problem more complex.'

Wayne lifted the typed notes that Lavers had brought. Lavers had been pretty busy, he saw. Lavers worked for a local company that manufactured office equipment — everything from filing systems to tabulators. Contrary to Wayne's first impressions, Lavers had been around in Darton City for quite a while. Three months to be exact. During that period he had met his sister twice. He had concluded that Mitzi was happy enough doing what she had chosen to do for a living. The girl hadn't shown any great enthusiasm over having her brother living in the same town. Lavers had said he suspected that Mitzi would rather he left her alone to her own devices. Had Lavers been in closer contact with his sister he might have been able to provide some leads on her intimate men-friends.

He was still studying the list of names

and addresses, and the clubs where Mitzi Laverick had worked, when the phone rang. Maggie lifted the receiver and spoke into it.

'Wayne Investigations! Yeah . . . Mr. Wayne is here. Mr. Cotter calling? I see . . . '

Wayne reached over and took the phone from Maggie. His pulse quickened when he heard Morton Cotter's voice.

'Hello again, Mr. Wayne.' The tone was cool and unruffled. Wayne tried guessing at what was on his mind.

'Hello yourself. I didn't think you'd remember me for this long, Mr. Cotter.'

Cotter's laugh was thin.

'I'd like to say that I'm sorry for what happened here when you called.'

'Think nothing of it. It was very useful experience. Now I know to whistle softly when I see a dog drooling. Now I know to shoot first at guys whose excess energy goes to their heads.'

'But I said that I'm sorry . . . '

'Yeah, you did. No hard feelings. Goodbye, Mr. Cotter.'

'No. Wait,' Cotter said. 'I've been

thinking over what happened to the girl — what did they call her — Mitzi Shaderick.'

'Laverick.'

'Well, it was something of the sort. It sounded like Mitzi Shaderick. I searched my memory to see if I remembered her at all.'

'And nothing came out?'

'Well, not much. But I was abrupt with you, Wayne. I'm not doing much at the minute, and I thought if you called — '

'The police will be glad to hear from you, Mr. Cotter,' Wayne said gently. 'Your apologies are accepted.'

'I understood you were working on the case,' Cotter said with an edge to his voice.

'Not in a dedicated fashion. I'm interested merely because I happened to be in the car with Miss Shaderick — beg pardon — Laverick, when it crashed.'

'Very unfortunate. You must have been shaken.'

'I'm still shaking.'

'If you don't wish to see me then . . . '

'It's not important. On the other hand,

if you insist on making amends with a drink of bourbon — '

'It's what you like, Mr. Wayne?'

'I'm in a mood for bourbon. I never let habits get a grip on me. Just when bourbon figures I'm hooked I switch to scotch. Psychology, if you know what I mean.'

Cotter said patiently, 'When can I expect you?'

'As soon as I make it there. But first of all, Mr. Cotter, I hope the Alsatian is locked up. I don't feel much like whistling at the minute.'

'I'll be waiting for you, Mr. Wayne,' Cotter rejoined tonelessly.

Wayne hung up and looked at Maggie Yarmon. Maggie was rubbing her fingers together. Her eyes glinted excitedly.

'You want to take a bet, Joey?'

'On Morton being our man? Don't let it throw you, Maggie. Mort Cotter is nothing but a very smooth guy. A call from a private eye and a police sergeant in the one afternoon upsets his astrologer's chart. He figures he needs to get back on the side of the angels. If the cops wanted to make it mean for him they've only to look in his direction.'

'And how do you know he doesn't just want you over there so he can feed you to the dog and be done with you?'

'There's the rub, baby. I don't know. If I can't make it back here inside an hour you can go out and toll a bell or something.'

Wayne was thoughtful on the ride to Columbus Avenue. Why would Cotter roll out the carpet if he didn't have a motive? A man like Mort Cotter didn't give a smile away without having the percentage angle weighed up.

There were only two cars parked at the front of the house on this trip. There was no sign of the Alsatian or the bald man who kept it in good humour. Wayne rang the bell and had a careless grin in place when the butler opened the door.

'Yes, sir!' he greeted in a dead voice. 'What can I do for you?'

'There's one crack has a faintly familiar ring. You haven't forgotten me so soon, I hope. If you say you have my ego's going to take a real beating.'

'If you'll let me have your card, sir, and tell me the nature of your visit.'

'Okay, pal. Play it any way you want it. I don't have a card, except a credit card would get me by maybe. My name is Joe Wayne and I have an appointment with a glass of bourbon. In Mr. Cotter's back room, that is.'

'Please come with me.'

He led Wayne into the hall. Wayne sat down on the pseudo-antique chair without waiting to be shown there. The butler continued round the bend in the hall. He returned in a moment and extended a finger.

'Mr. Cotter will see you now, sir. He's waiting in the library.'

'How about Nate and Rod? Are they waiting in the nearest shadow?'

'Really, Mr. Wayne!'

'Really yourself,' Wayne grunted and walked past him. The third door on his right was open. It led into a room that could have served as a convention chamber. Two walls were lined from floor to ceiling with books. On another wall a single painting hung. It was hanging by itself on account of there not being enough space left to take a postage stamp.

A huge davenport occupied the side of the room that offered a generous view of the lawns and tennis courts. Four easy chairs were spaced on the sombre black and brown carpeting. On one of them Morton Cotter sat, occasional table near by. The table had an array of bottles, glasses, shakers and ice bucket.

'Well, here we are, Mr. Wayne!'

Cotter rose lithely and extended a hand. His grip was firm, with just the merest suggestion of moistness. Even so, Wayne was tempted to wipe his own hand when he took it away.

'It was good of you to see me.'

Wayne heard the door clicking shut and glanced across his shoulder. The butler had wanted to make sure the meeting was a peacable one before leaving.

'Sit down. Make yourself comfortable.' Cotter smiled and it lent a cunning to his eyes. 'As you can see, I've got your favourite drink laid on.'

'You shouldn't have taken the trouble.' Wayne took the chair opposite to

Cotter and the night club owner fixed two drinks. As he drank Wayne's gaze roamed over the huge room. He had the feeling that other eyes were watching them and other ears listening in. Cotter's mouth curled in what was supposed to be an amused smile.

'You look kind of nervous, Mr. Wayne. Don't worry. Nobody will kill you unless I give the word.'

Wayne nearly choked on his bourbon. Cotter's laugh worked on his spine like a coarse file. His stomach went into a tight knot and it took an effort to get it to relax.

'That makes a very neat joke, if your taste happens to run to the macabre.'

'I'm not joking, friend. I never concoct gags so early in the day. My imaginative processes take a long time in warming up.'

'Please warn me when they do. I'd really like to be the other side of town when you're being creative.'

Cotter took a sip from his glass and set it on the table. He brought a cigar from a leather case and lit it with the delicacy of an artist applying a brush stroke. When he had the cigar burning to his satisfaction he pointed a rigid finger at his guest.

'You're a private snooper, friend. You happened to be hired by some dame that was in trouble. The dame was in enough trouble to get herself killed. You learned that she was a singer, that she'd worked at one of my clubs. You put two and one together and got yourself four. Do I make myself clear?'

'You make yourself very offensive.'

'Don't hand me that guff, mister. Mugs in your line give me a large pain. You act smart when nobody stops you. You go into hysterics when you meet opposition. You've met opposition, pal. Right now. You'll meet more opposition if you don't lift your clumsy foot from my neck. That's your kind of language, isn't it?'

'Ain't it,' Wayne said slowly. He placed his glass on the floor. He rose to his feet and turned to the door of the room. 'What happens when I open it? Do I get a pack of wolves or do you just have a guy killed cleanly with a knife?'

'You get nothing when you walk out of

the door, chum. You get everything if you try to come back. I thought I'd bring you here so there would be no possible misunderstanding. I don't play cops and robbers with you punks. I never play with murder.'

'And you're not even strong on accidents?' Wayne murmured.

Cotter was lunging from the chair when he opened the door and headed for the sunlight. A dog wailed mournfully as he reached the Plymouth and got the motor turning.

8

At nine that evening Wayne sat at the bar of the Jackpot Club and played with the bourbon which the bartender had placed before him.

There were few other customers at the bar just then, as the high spot of the evening was about to commence. Waiters traded between the tables scattered across the wide floor area and the two drink fixers who worked expertly and swiftly.

The lights were dim and the air-conditioning was terrible. Wayne scanned the sea of faces and thought that humanity would be a wonderful thing when it caught up with itself.

He was bringing his glass to his lips when a tall blonde in a low-cut black dress came onto the stage to the introductory tinkle of the pianist. She bowed and smiled, giving her audience their dollar's worth of well-developed bosom before straightening to a ripple of applause.

The orchestra lifted her voice carefully. It was the kind of voice that demanded respect, Wayne decided. He didn't know enough about voices to be an expert, but he liked what he heard. He thought about nothing but the blonde's singing until she finished her number. She bowed again and smiled again. She threw kisses that brought a few wolf whistles from the tables. Wayne heard somebody having his face smacked. Then the blonde retreated gracefully to a door leading off-stage.

A male singer with crew-cut hair style and all the self-confidence he needed took over the spotlight. He wore a large carnation in his buttonhole and wriggled his body as he went into a current pop rave.

'Like a hangover after a night out compared with Sally,' the bartender observed to nobody in particular. He happened to be looking in Wayne's direction when he said it. He sighed and gathered up empty glasses.

'Sally is the blonde,' Wayne said. 'Her

other name is Rogan, isn't it?'

The bartender noticed Wayne then and frowned slightly. 'That's right,' he said distantly. 'But don't get steamed up over it.'

'I don't steam that easy. Keep the fire extinguisher for somebody else.'

Wayne finished his drink and lit a cigarette. He waited until the bartender was engaged before circling the room and slipping through the back-stage door.

Here was a dim corridor with as much character as a flat beer. Wayne's eyes searched for the dressing-room bearing Sally Rogan's name. The names were blocked in pencil and the labels could be dispensed within five seconds after a performer moved on. Mitzi Laverick had moved on, Wayne thought sadly. He wished he could be sure it was Dell Lavers's retainer driving him; he hated to think of his conscience providing the sole motivation.

He tapped on the door bearing the blonde's label, then gripped the handle and turned it without waiting for an answer. The lock was off and he stepped into the room.

Sally Rogan was seated at her dressing-table, chin resting on the palms of her hands, gazing pensively at her reflection in the mirror. She frowned at Wayne, stooped without speaking, and took off one of her high-heeled shoes.

'I'm sorry, honey. I'm not the boots. What are you going to do with that?'

The blonde balanced the shoe in her right hand.

'See how fast that silly grin can leave your face. Go on, buster, save your bouquet for somebody else who might appreciate it.'

'Mitzi Laverick?'

The blood drained from the singer's cheeks, leaving them pale and tense. She lowered the shoe and turned slightly on her chair. 'Who — who are you? That was a terrible thing to say. Don't you know that Mitzi is dead?'

'I do, honey. I agree with you. I don't intend any harm. I'm Joe Wayne. I'm interested in what happened to Mitzi. You were a friend of hers?'

The blonde looked at him for a long moment without saying anything. Her eyelashes fluttered.

'Sure I was. But what do you know about it? How is it any of your business? Oh, I get it! The police . . . '

She started to put her shoe on. She froze with her head bent when Wayne went on grinning. Anxiety crept in.

'Not exactly, Sally. You haven't talked with the police?'

She straightened jerkily and said no. 'If you're not from the police, who are you?' she added.

'A private investigator. Mitzi's brother hired me to ask around. I heard this was the last joint she worked at, so I took a chance.'

'I see!'

The blonde moved her head to look at the mirror. She seemed to be examining her lipstick. Her face was calm when she looked at Wayne.

'A chance on what?' she asked curiously.

'Getting a little co-operation, Sally. I need pieces. You might have one;

somebody else might have one. It's how I operate. I collect and go on collecting until I can fit the pieces so they make some sense.'

The blonde assimilated that. She nodded slowly to let Wayne know she understood.

'I was sitting here, thinking about her. This was her dressing-room. I feel like her ghost is hiding right there in the closet. It was a terrible end.'

'Then you'd be willing to help me?'

Wayne moved on into the room. Cheap perfume. Shoddy furniture that might have been something in the gay twenties. A lino square on the floorboards. If ghosts were hovering here it was no wonder. He thought of Morton Cotter, sitting at home in his swank library. Surrounded by his books and his guard dogs. He took out a pack of cigarettes and offered the girl one. She held her lips and he inserted the cigarette gently.

'You've got a nice mouth. It reminds me of kissing.'

The blonde shrugged. Her shoulders hadn't seen a lot of the sun. 'I bet you say that to all the girls. Look, Mr. Wayne, if I were you I'd be very nervous around now.'

'I'm weak at the knees. I wondered what was wrong.'

'Chris Corby. He's the manager. He'd have a fit if he caught you here. I'm on again in five minutes too. I wish I could help you. I was fond of Mitzi. I'm sorry I can't.'

Wayne thought she was too definite about that too soon. It started him wondering.

'We could talk elsewhere,' he suggested. 'Later. What time do you quit?'

The girl hesitated, puffing at the cigarette. 'I'm not so sure,' she said finally.

'Of what — that I'm not one hundred per cent honourable and in complete command of my impulses? Please, Miss Rogan! Or can I call you Sally?'

'But how could I help you?' she protested. 'I can't see how I could.'

'Let me figure it out, Sally. All I want is a talk about Mitzi. I promise to make it short and painless. So what time do you get through?'

'I finish early tonight. At eleven.' She said it slowly and hesitantly. She studied him closely.

'How about me picking you up and seeing you home? If you can't bring yourself to trust me, I can get you a chaperone. My secretary. Sober. Staid. She beats me over the head if I even mention dames.'

Sally Rogan laughed softly. Her eyes twinkled on Wayne's. 'All right. But don't worry about your secretary. I think I can trust you.'

'Swell. I'll be at the front at what time — eleven?'

'I usually take a cab home. It'll save me the trouble.'

'Where is home anyhow, Sally?'

'Mendoza Drive. Twelve, fifteen. It's an apartment house. Now you'd better leave before — '

At that instant the door was rapped crisply and opened. A stout man with a flabby face and small eyes looked in. His mouth sagged when he saw Wayne.

'What's going on here, Sally?' he

demanded querulously. 'You know the rules here as well as the next person — '

'Blame me,' Joe Wayne grinned. 'I happened to run into an old friend of Sally. She asked me to drop by and say hello for her. I'm sorry if I was breaking any rules.'

'I see.' The small eyes were bleak and suspicious. They switched to the blonde and became reproachful. 'But all the same, Sally, you should have warned him.'

'But she did,' Wayne explained. 'I'm just going. So-long for now, Sally.'

'Goodbye, Mr. Wayne. Thank you for calling.'

The fat man stepped to one side to let Wayne leave the room. Wayne threw him a salute on the way past. He closed the door behind him and stood for a moment. Chris Corby's voice rose shrilly.

'You know damn well what the boss would say — '

'Stuff the boss,' Sally Rogan told the fat man. 'Stuff you too. And say another word to me and I'll walk off and leave you flat.'

'I'm sorry, Sally! I didn't mean it that way, but . . . ' Wayne moved off without listening to any more.

★　★　★

At five minutes before eleven he cruised to the front of the Jackpot Club and stalled the engine. There was a fine rain falling that made the neons tawdry somehow. Few pedestrians were about. The vestibule of the club looked empty and forlorn. Wayne stifled a yawn and poked a cigarette to his mouth.

He was drawing a light to it when he noticed somebody move under the neons and approach his car. The man wore a uniform and he guessed it was the doorman.

'Are you Mr. Wayne?'

'That's right,' Wayne said. 'I'm waiting for Miss Rogan.'

'I know. She got through earlier than she expected. She said you'd know where to see her.'

'Thanks. Say, who told you to pass on the message?'

'Sally told the boss. The boss told me to watch for you.' The man poked his head close to the car to escape the rain. He looked closely at Wayne.

'By boss you mean Mr. Corby?'

'That's right.'

'Thanks.'

The man stood on and Wayne got the message. He fingered out a bill and glanced at it. A dollar.

'Don't spend it all in the one bar.'

'Thank *you*, Mr. Wayne. Good hunting.'

Wayne engaged gear and drove off. The rain was thickening and he switched on the screen wipers. So Sally had finished sooner than she'd thought she would. That was all right by him, but he wished she could have told the doorman without letting Corby know. If Corby was supicious he might mention his interest in Sally to Mort Cotter.

It was a fifteen-minute journey from the club to Mendoza Drive. He pulled up short of the apartment house that was numbered 1215, locked the car and went into the lobby to read the listings. Sally

Rogan was in 312. The elevator was self-service and Wayne thumbed out at the third floor.

He walked along to 312 and rang the doorbell. When nobody answered he frowned, wondering if Sally had decided to drop off somewhere else before coming home. He rang again and tried the door handle. The door opened under his pressure and he stepped into the lighted room.

Sally Rogan wasn't in the apartment; two men were. They sat on chairs against the wall, cigarettes in their mouths. One of them wore a black fedora; his companion wore a Tyrolean hat. Neither of them looked surprised. Both of them looked as though they might have been waiting for something to happen — such as a visitor like Joe Wayne turning up.

Wayne hid his anxiety and said, 'Hi there. Sally didn't mention there was going to be a party.'

'Who are you?' the man nearest to Wayne said. He was short and stocky, and wore a trench coat over a light grey suit. By contrast his companion was tallish and thin, with a faint scar on his right cheek that could have been caused by a knife blade. This one removed the cigarette from his mouth and rubbed at his nose.

'Okay, pal, we're waiting. Who are you? What are you doing at Sally Rogan's apartment?'

'Then it is Sally's place after all. For a minute there I figured I'd walked into the wrong apartment.'

'That could be as you say, pal,' the man with the scar said. 'You might have rambled into the wrong apartment.'

'But if Sally lives here — '

'Sally does live here,' the stocky man said curtly. 'Answer the question.'

'My name is Joe Wayne. My friends just call me Joe,' he added with a wry grin. 'But judging by the weight of the atmosphere I'd be making a mistake if I called you guys my friends.'

'Let's find out about it,' the thin man said. 'You forgot to close the door. Close it.'

Wayne hesitated. The pair were obviously a pair of hoodlums. They had been planted to persuade him he ought to have left Sally Rogan alone. But where was Sally? Had she arranged this set-up for him?

He backed carefully to the door and closed it. Neither of the two had moved in his chair. The stocky man pointed to a chair by a small table.

'Take the weight off your feet. It's raining outside?'

'It's been raining for the past hour. No, thanks, I don't think I'll be staying after all. It was Sally I wanted to see here — '

'What for?'

Wayne laughed shortly. 'Come off it, boys. You don't expect me to tell you what's between me and Sally.'

'What is between you and Sally anyhow?' the thin man said.

'Our own business. Where is Sally?'

'Let's get this straight, pal. We do the asking and you do the telling. Okay?'

'If you don't waste much of my time.'

'Sit down then. Make yourself at home.'

Wayne slid onto the edge of the chair. It was a signal for the stocky man to come to his feet. He did it effortlessly for a man of his bulk. He dropped his cigarette to the floor and put his shoe on it.

'Sally's going to be mad at you for spoiling the rug.'

The stocky man took a step towards Wayne. His fleshy face was completely deadpan; only his eyes conveyed what Wayne read as the threat of menace.

'You're quite a wit, aren't you? What do you use when your brains take a powder?'

His shoe was racing at Wayne's ankle when Wayne threw himself out of the chair. He rolled into the small table and knocked it over. The stocky man grunted and reached for him. His companion's laugh was a dry rasp.

'You're gonna have fun, Charley.'

Charley kicked at Wayne again. Wayne drew back and thrust his right hand under his coat. The thin man spoke warningly.

'Don't! You're covered . . . '

Wayne surged up, head tucked down, neck and shoulders braced for shock. He connected with the stocky man's midriff and sent the wind out of him. The stocky man grunted.

'He's cute.'

'He's giving you a race, Charley.'

A fist like a slab of rock took Wayne in the side of the neck. He whirled and was trapped by iron fingers that ground into his right arm.

'I'm going to break it up, sonny. How many pieces?'

Wayne sent the ridged fingers of his left hand at the stocky man's groin. This time he found a soft spot. Eyes bulged and hot breath smote Wayne's cheek He dragged his arm free and chopped at the man's nose. Blood spouted. Wayne made an axe with his hand and chopped again, frantically and without mercy. A final kick to the ribs put the stocky man to the floor.

The gun in the thin man's hand erupted as Wayne raced at him. It was fitted with a silencer and made a sharp popping sound. The noise of the bullet striking the wall at the door was much louder. Wayne closed with him before he could trigger twice. He grappled for the gun hand, twisted it. The gun fell to the floor. When the thin man went after it

Wayne tramped on his spread fingers. The man screamed.

Wayne brought both fists together, making a hammer now. He threw all his weight and strength into the downswing. The clenched fists made a dull explosion on the crown of the thin man's head. The fedora crumpled. Wayne bent over him to repeat the manoeuvre if necessary. The man groaned and flopped over onto his back. His mouth opened and his eyes rolled.

Wayne straightened and went through the rest of the rooms. Sally Rogan wasn't here. Something had happened to Sally Rogan too, that or she had sold him out.

He gathered up his hat and pulled it onto his head. Then with a final glance at the pair he left the apartment, closing the door firmly behind him.

He was lucky enough to meet no one on his way to the elevator. He rode to ground level and paused in the lobby for a few minutes to look up and down the street. Everything was quiet. He hurried back to the Plymouth and slumped behind the wheel. He opened the window and sat dragging air to his lungs. The rain beat in at him. He didn't mind.

He was lighting a cigarette when a cab drew in at the front of the apartment house. A girl got out and paid off the driver. She didn't glance to right or left before dashing into the lobby.

Wayne wondered grimly what it was all about.

9

Ten minutes dragged by before a man emerged from the apartment building. He wasn't too steady on his feet and Wayne recognised him as Charley. His thin companion came at his heels. They stood in the rain and had a short conversation. It ended with them walking a hundred yards to a parked car.

Charley opened the driving side door and flopped under the wheel. The thin man peered through the rain and then got into the car also. The engine started and the car moved off.

It had been Wayne's intention to go up and have it out with Sally Rogan straightaway; he changed his mind now. When the car in front drew near to the end of the street Wayne took the Plymouth after it.

He expected the car to set out for Morton Cotter's place on Columbus Avenue; it went into the opposite direction instead. Some movie houses were erupting and here and there was a traffic clutter. Twice Wayne thought he had lost the car, but he picked it up again and stepped on the gas.

Twenty minutes later the car went round the Dormann Buildings and turned into Huxley Park. Huxley Park was close to the southern fringe of Darton City. It was a high-class district, and didn't fit the background that Wayne had painted for Charley and the thin man.

He slowed the Plymouth when he saw the other car slowing. Suddenly the other car veered sharply to the right and went from view. It could be a ruse, he knew. They might have known he was following them and wished to create confusion. He trod on the accelerator all the same, not taking his eye off the spot where the car had vanished.

He braked close to the kerb and stuck his head out of the window. Here was a driveway that curved to the front of a large house. As Wayne watched he saw headlights being cut. Lamps glowed up there, but the house was too far to be able to see clearly what was happening.

He reversed carefully until he was a safe distance from the driveway entrance and yet close enough to see the car when it emerged once more. He had seen the name of the house on a sign at the entrance. *Montcalm.* He thought it queer the names people gave houses. He wondered who the muscle boys were visiting. He wondered if their visit would be a lengthy one.

A quarter of an hour passed, half an hour. Ten minutes after that Wayne concluded that the pair might live at *Montcalm*. It was a strange world, as Ripley had discovered. But there didn't seem to be much sense in hanging around for any longer.

He waited until the road was clear and made a U-turn, then drove steadily for Mendoza Drive again.

He parked a hundred yards past the apartment building where Sally Rogan lived. On his feet he scanned the shadows with a keen eye. The rain had slackened and the sky was clearing. A siren wailed on the night. It was a long way off, but the sound always did something to Wayne's nerves.

As before, the lobby was deserted. The elevator rested at ground level. He went into the cage and thumbed for the third floor. A door opened as he stepped out and a pale-faced woman stared at him.

'Are you the police?'

She had her hair in curlers and wore a dressing-robe. A cold fist hit Wayne in the stomach.

'The police? Is something the matter?'

'I guess so. I heard a commotion along there a little while ago. It seemed to come from three, twelve.'

Wayne smiled.

'Forget it, lady. I am the police. I had a message. Somebody else must have been disturbed. Don't worry.'

'I can't help worrying. I live here alone.'

Wayne smiled again and waited until she retreated into her own apartment and closed the door. The smile faded from his mouth as he walked on to 312 and rang the bell. Nothing stirred and he gripped the door handle and turned it. The door was locked this trip. He rang the bell again.

'Who is it?' Sally Rogan's voice.

'It's me, honey. Good old Joe.'

'But it's so late now . . . Couldn't you come back tomorrow, Mr. Wayne?'

'See here, baby, it's now or never. If you won't let me in tonight, you might have the cops calling tomorrow. Besides which, Sally, folks on this floor are wondering what's wrong.'

'Very well.'

The door was unlocked and opened. When Sally Rogan saw the .38 in Wayne's hand her mouth curved to scream.

'Hold it, Sally. You'll only disturb the whole building.'

She covered her mouth with her hands and stepped back to allow him to enter. He entered cautiously and heard the door being closed behind him. He turned to look at the girl.

'It's quite all right. I'm just being careful. Stay where you are until I get back.'

Sally Rogan only made a gurgling

sound in her throat when he left her to search the rooms. He returned to find her sitting on the couch, a glass of something held tightly in her hands. She had a frightened gleam in her eyes.

'Did you lock the door, honey?'

She nodded and took a drink from her glass. Even when Wayne slid the .38 into its sheath she showed no signs of relaxing.

'What — what happened?' she gasped finally.

'Tell me, baby.'

Wayne took the chair opposite her. He noticed that the table had been turned the right way up; there was no evidence of Charley's cigarette on the rug. He brought his gaze to bear squarely on the girl.

'I — I don't understand . . . ' she said weakly.

'We could form some kind of team maybe.'

Sally Rogan laid her glass down and got a cigarette going. Her fingers trembled as did her lips when she puffed rapidly.

'When I got home I found these

men — ' she began and broke off.

'No kidding? How many — three, four? A gal like you is bound to have lots of admirers.'

'You won't believe me!' she cried in a hurt voice. 'It's true, I tell you, Mr. Wayne. When I came in here there were two men. They looked as though they had been fighting. One of them was on the floor. The other was making him take a drink.'

'But you recognised them straight off, of course.'

'What! Are you crazy? I never saw them before in my life. And — ' She broke off to stare hard at Wayne. 'Did you know they were here?'

'How would I know, honey? I'm just a guy that asks questions. I don't make a habit of breaking up private shindigs. Tell me all about it. Then I'll ask you why you didn't turn up to be brought home when you said you would.'

'I can explain that — '

'Later will do. Let's stick to the horrified shock when you discovered Tweedledum and Tweedledee resolving to have a battle.'

'You know more about it than you pretend to know,' she accused. 'What the hell is going on anyhow?' she added heatedly.

Wayne considered her for ten seconds. He coaxed a grin to his lips. 'It's why I'm asking, Sally. And do remember that I'm on your side and not theirs.'

'Theirs!'

It was another moment when Wayne thought she would scream. He lifted the bottle she had been using and poured a splash into her glass. He handed her the glass.

'Swallow it up.'

'Theirs!' she repeated. 'Tell me what you mean? Are you referring to the car crash that Mitzi had?'

'I'm not sure, Sally. I don't know what fits and what doesn't. I would advise you to come clean with me about tonight.'

'But I told you — '

'Okay. You told me. You came home and found two men in your apartment. You didn't know them?'

'How many times do I say it! I didn't

know them. I didn't ask them to be here when I got home. You were supposed to pick me up at the club.'

'We'll reach that presently, Sally. Take it from where you arrived home. Didn't it occur to you to phone for the police when you saw your place had been broken into?'

'Of course it did. It was the first thing I decided to do. Then they started to explain. At least one of them did.'

'Which one?'

'He was tall and had — Well, it looked like a scar on his face. He apologised. He said that he and his friend had come to the wrong apartment building. His friend had been drinking too much. So had he, he said. Then they argued and fought. He took twenty dollars from his wallet and left it there on the TV. He said it would cover any damage that had been done.'

'You believed them?'

'I couldn't make up my mind. The other man said I'd better grab the money and forget it. They took off before I could gather my wits.'

Wayne walked over to the TV set.

Somebody had left four fives there right enough. The whole set-up was getting more complicated by the minute. Wayne poured a drink for himself and resumed his chair. Sally Rogan was attempting to drink too and her teeth rattled against the glass.

'I'm too scared about the whole thing now, Mr. Wayne,' she quavered. 'Please go away and leave me alone. I don't want to get mixed up in trouble. Mitzi must have been in trouble. Otherwise why was she killed?'

'It's what I want to find out,' Wayne said patiently. 'I've got to talk with you, Sally. You've got to tell me anything you know.'

'You go on like a parrot,' she cried impatiently. 'Anything I know! I don't know anything. Can I make myself plainer?'

Wayne dragged air to his lungs. It was a stand-in for air — a mixture of cigarette smoke, liquor fumes, stale perfume.

'All the same, Sally,' he said reasonably. 'It's got to be me or the police. I'm not police, but I'm operating alongside them.

First of all,' he continued before she interrupted him, 'you were to see me at eleven. You didn't make it at eleven. You were supposed to have gone home early.'

'Who told you that?' the girl snapped.

'The doorman did. He said you'd gotten through earlier than you'd expected. He said I'd know where to find you.'

'But that — that's a downright . . . ' She ran flat on that and trapped her tongue in her teeth. Twin flushes of colour stained her cheeks. 'I'm not saying another word, Mr. Wayne,' she blurted after a moment. 'Now will you please go?'

'It's what you want?' Wayne asked evenly.

'It's what I want.' She switched her gaze away from him, appeared to concentrate on a spot on the opposite wall. Her bosom rose and fell quickly.

'Okay, Sally. I guess I can't drag it out of you if you've made up your mind.'

Wayne drained his glass and laid it on the table. He walked to the door of the apartment. Sally Rogan talked rapidly behind him.

'You must understand, Mr. Wayne. I'm not going to get involved in anything. I don't want to get involved. I — I don't want to be found dead . . . '

'I don't want you to be found dead, Sally.' Wayne twisted the door handle. 'But you'll be wasting your time if you go straight to bed when I leave. I'll be back soon, and not alone.'

She looked horrified. 'You intend to bring the police!'

'What else can I do? I'm convinced you know more about Mitzi Laverick than you're willing to admit. And you will admit that you played me for a sucker tonight. You had that doorman give me a message. I arrived here in good faith, but what did I find?'

'You — you were here when those men — '

Wayne nodded. 'They weren't drunk. They were as sober as two judges. But they were a lot meaner than two judges. If I hadn't made sure to have my vitamins this morning you'd have found me here instead of them. And in a very sorry plight too, I might add.'

152

He opened the door and stepped out. Sally Rogan bounced up and called to him.

'No, Mr. Wayne! Wait. I can explain about tonight. I haven't got a thing to hide.'

'I wish I could say that, Sally. And call me Joe.' He closed the door and went back to his chair. The girl sank down opposite him.

'I should have got through at eleven tonight,' she began. 'It turned out that an act didn't arrive on time. The boss asked me to take over.'

'Chris Corby? What time did he ask?'

'Just as I was preparing to dress for the street. I said I was sorry and had a date waiting for me.'

'Mentioning my name?'

'Well, I — I gave him the line that you gave him when he walked in on us in my dressing-room tonight. I said you were a friend of a friend and had promised to take me out.'

'Uhuh!' Wayne urged when she stopped talking. 'Then what? You left, but gave me the slip?'

'Of course I didn't. When an emergency crops up you're expected to pitch in. What else could I do?'

'What else?' Wayne echoed. He had the feeling that all he was doing here was wasting time. 'But you're forgetting that the doorman told me you'd quit earlier and had gone home.'

'If he said so he was telling a lie.'

'He said the boss told him to pass your message on to me, Sally.'

'But why would Corby play such a trick?' Her eyes widened. 'You don't suppose that Chris Corby actually kept me behind on purpose, that he arranged to have those two men . . . Oh, no!'

'Why not, honey? How well do you know Chris Corby?'

'What has that got to do with it?' the girl demanded. She poked her thumbnail at her teeth. 'I'm getting more scared by the minute,' she confessed hoarsely. 'Mr. Wayne, please . . . Be a good guy and leave me alone.'

'In a minute. Let's drop Corby for the present, Sally. Let's concentrate on you.'

'Me? But — '

'How long have you worked at the Jackpot Club?'

'A couple of months.'

'Mitzi Laverick worked there when you joined?'

'Yes, she did. I got along swell with Mitzi. I thought I had a future as a singer until I heard Mitzi sing.'

'Don't underrate yourself. I thought you were great.'

'For how much longer?' Sally Rogan said bitterly. 'And why can't people leave me alone?'

'Do you know who owns the Jackpot Club?' Wayne asked her.

'Mr. Cotter owns it. He owns a lot of clubs.'

'But the Jackpot is the first one of his you worked for, Sally?'

'As far as I know. Yes, I do know. What are you driving at? You're barking up the wrong tree.'

'You could be right. To get back to Mitzi now, honey. Did she have many friends?'

'You mean boy-friends, of course?'

'I was thinking of boy-friends, more or

less. She was a nice girl. She must have had plenty of guys around.'

'Will you get me another drink?'

Wayne fixed her another drink. After the second pull from the glass more colour came into the girl's cheeks.

'I shouldn't be drinking this late. I'll have a terrible head in the morning. Look, Mr. Wayne, maybe we ought to get the police after all. I'm getting scared now when I think of those men, and the lies that Corby and the doorman told. Harry knew I was still at the club, so why did he tell you I wasn't?'

'I thought we'd settled that, Sally. Your boss told him to do it. Harry likes eating, I guess. There's no need to get the police unless you're really scared.'

'But I might be in danger too. And a minute ago you were all for calling the police.'

'If you talk to me you don't need talk to them. To get back to my question, honey: did Mitzi have any steady men-friends?'

The girl thought hard for a few moments. It was plain that she had drunk more than she normally did. She had been shocked to find the two men in her apartment when she arrived home, distressed when she learned that the pair had really been waiting for Wayne to turn up to give him a beating. Now she was confused and frightened — not an ideal state to be in when clear answers were required.

'Yes,' she said finally. 'There was a man called Harold. He was a nice looking guy and used to come to the club for no other reason than to watch Mitzi and be near her.'

'When did you see this Harold last?'

'Oh, let me see . . . A week ago, I'd say.'

'Did you know his full name?'

'Mitzi told me. His name is Ypson.'

'Thanks, honey. Any idea where he hangs out?'

She shook her head. 'Mitzi didn't tell me if she knew. I do know she was out with Ypson. It's all I know about him. I don't think it's possible he would have harmed Mitzi.'

'You're a doll, Sally,' Wayne said warmly. 'That's everything you can think of at the moment?'

'Everything. Now will you please go and leave me alone?'

'Sure. But before I do . . . ' Wayne took a card from his wallet and laid it on the table. 'If you want to see me again, Sally, or if you think you need help, just ring that number. If I'm not at home leave a message.'

'All right. I'll do that. But what do I say to Mr. Corby if he asks me about tonight?'

'Not a thing. Don't mention me. If he mentions the toughs you found here, tell him what they told you. They were drunk and lost their way.'

Wayne held her hand for a moment and turned to the door. He smiled and said so-long before going out.

When the door closed behind him Sally Rogan burst into tears.

10

Wayne awakened early next morning. He showered, shaved, dressed in a brown suit that had seen better days. He had breakfast on his way to the Wilton Buildings. Early as he was, Maggie Yarmon was at the back of her desk when he walked into the office.

'Hello there, Sunshine,' Maggie greeted breezily. 'How did last evening go?'

'So-so,' Wayne told her. He perched on the desk beside Maggie and looked at her crisp white blouse.

'What the Sam Hill are you doing that for?'

'I'm thinking,' Wayne told her.

'Oh, yeah! Well just think about something else for a change. Guys like you have only one reason for staying alive. It's positively disgusting. A girl's not safe anywhere any more. Did you find out who killed Mitzi Laverick?'

Wayne shook his head, grinning wryly.

He lit a cigarette and put it in Maggie's mouth. He lit another one and puffed at it. He told Maggie to check through the phone book for the name of the resident of a house called *Montcalm* on Huxley Park.

'Are you kidding, Joey? What's the matter with calling Information on the phone and asking them?'

'Do it my way, baby. I don't want any nasty repercussions so early in the day.'

Maggie shrugged and opened the directory. Wayne lifted the phone and rang Sally Rogan's apartment. It seemed a long time before he had an answer.

'Yes . . . What is it?'

'This is Joe, Sally. You know the Joe I'm talking about. I hope you had a good night's sleep.'

'None of your fault if she hadn't,' Maggie Yarmon lifted her head to hiss. 'When do you put any work in?'

'Is something the matter, Mr. Wayne?' Sally Rogan asked with a catch to her voice.

'No, Sally. I just wondered if you'd

remembered anything more that you forgot to tell me last night.'

'I wish you'd leave me alone, Mr. Wayne. I really do. I don't want to get involved.'

'All right, Sally. Thanks anyhow. If you do come up with a bright idea, you'll let me have it?'

Sally Rogan's answer was an inaudible grunt. She hung up and Wayne sighed.

'There's a bad smell hanging around Mort Cotter and his Jackpot Club.' He remembered the name that Sally had given him last night. He went into his own office and pulled over the phone book. There were few Ypson listed; one of them had the initials J.H. He dialled that number and after a moment had a sleepy reply.

'Yeah! Jack Ypson here.'

'Jack Ypson? I wanted to speak to a Harold Ypson. You wouldn't have a brother?'

He heard a short laugh. 'I guess you're thinking about me. My friends usually call me Harold.'

'Fine!'

'What do you mean, fine? Who are you anyhow?'

'My name is Wayne. Joseph Wayne. I'd like to see you as soon as possible, Harold.'

'Are you the police?'

Wayne frowned while he hesitated. Was it possible that the cops had already been over this ground? It showed that Hank Petersen really worked hard to earn his reputation.

'I'm not the police. I'm a private investigator. Perhaps it'll give you a clue as to the nature of my inquiries.'

It was Ypson's turn to hesitate now. He said slowly, 'Are you talking about Mitzi Laverick?'

'I'm talking about Mitzi Laverick. Her brother hired me in connection with her death. By the way, Harold, have the police been with you?'

'Why should they? There's nothing I could say that would be of any help.'

The man's voice had risen to a pitch verging on alarm.

'Let me decide that, Harold. I'm on my way to your place now. Please don't go off until I arrive.'

'But you can't — '

Wayne replaced the receiver and went out to Maggie. Maggie had made a note on a slip of paper.

'That was easier than I figured it would be. Times I think I've got extra sensory perception. You're in for a surprice, I believe, Joey.'

'How come?' Wayne lifted the slip of paper and stared. F. L. Cotter, he read. 'Well what do you know!'

'I thought it might throw you, Joe. So there's more than one of the family in town. Funny our files had nothing on him. But they had very little on Morton, when you come to think about it. This Cotter clan might have a big yen to stay out of the limelight. How did you get the address anyhow?'

Briefly Wayne told her of last night's events. When he had finished Maggie whistled softly.

'So Morton keeps Alsatians and a lot of nasty tricks in the library. And F.L. keeps two chumps who didn't want you to talk with Sally Rogan. There you are, Joey!

Just like I spelled it out at the beginning. Mort Cotter's in this up to his two ears. His brother as well, likely . . . Did I say brother? Hell, my thinking machine's even giving out with inspirations this morning.'

'He could be a brother. He could also be a third cousin. Even a son. And there's just the slimmest of chances that they have nothing in common but their name.'

'Don't you believe it, Joe. You're making hot-shots all over the place. But shouldn't you tell Hank Petersen, just to be on the safe side in case of accidents?'

'If I get involved in an accident, you can tell Hank, baby. Right now I'm off to see this Harold Ypson. He sounds like a guy would scream murder at the drop of your bonnet.'

Wayne was at the door when the phone rang. He waited while Maggie lifted the receiver and spoke.

'Wayne Investigations here . . . Yeah! Hello again, Mr. Lavers. You want to talk with Joe? Anything new?'

Maggie covered the mouthpiece and

shook her head. Wayne gave her a thumbs down sign and left the office.

★　★　★

J. H. Ypson lived at a small house on the corner of Rutledge and Davison. It took Wayne a half hour to find the place. When he did he parked close to a sagging picket fence and opened a gate that creaked a lament. The district was right on the fringe of the skid-row locality, and as he walked up the short path to the front door he noticed eyes watching him from the window of the neighbouring house. He grinned and the eyes went away. He lifted an iron knocker and rattled it a couple of times. He was about to repeat the manoeuvre when the door opened suddenly and a young man stood there.

'Hello,' he said nervously. 'I guess you would be Mr. Wayne.'

'That's right,' Wayne said.

Ypson was dark and handsome. He was dressed in neat grey pants and cream sweater. There was an air of quiet frustration about him that Wayne found

165

interesting if not intriguing. He held the door open for Wayne to enter, then put his head out to look around him before closing the door and gesturing along a narrow hall.

'What was that for?'

Ypson coloured and grew more uncomfortable. 'I was thinking you might be a policeman after all.'

'I'm not a policeman. Would you like to look at my credentials so you can relax?'

'That would be a good idea,' Ypson allowed.

He examined the photostat that Wayne produced. He smiled wanly, then pointed to an open door.

The room had started out as somewhere to live in the evenings when the day's work was done. At the minute it was being used as an artist's studio. Sketches and paintings were everywhere, not the stuff that Wayne expected to be hung on walls, but the kind of nightmares that leap out of newspapers. The sort that say something is the best in the world to eat, or something else is the best way to keep your teeth white and dazzling.

'Wait till Ruth hears about this.'

'You must forgive the chaos,' Ypson apologised. 'There's a chair by the wall if you'd care to sit down.'

There really was a chair by the wall when Wayne lifted a couple of sacks and a bundle of wrapping paper. He sat down on it and looked at the creation coming to birth on an easel.

'So you're an artist, Harold. I have a friend who is an artist too.'

'Really? Commercial work like this?'

'In a way.' Wayne decided to skip it. If he started talking about Ruth Foran he might go on all day. Besides, he never talked about Ruth with anyone.

'I had a job with an agency,' Ypson explained. 'The head artist is a bastard. Everything I dreamed up he stifled in the cradle. I cut my losses and came home to work. I get an idea and sell it to the highest bidder.'

'That sounds cute,' Wayne murmured while he put a cigarette to his lips. 'How is it coming along?'

'Not very well, I'm afraid. But it takes

time for a revolutionary project to catch on. I decided to take the day off. I decided to walk for an hour or so. I get lots of ideas when I'm just walking around.'

'I won't keep you, Harold,' Wayne said carefully. 'You know why I'm calling. I wanted to find out how much you know about Mitzi Laverick.'

Ypson passed fingers over his handsome head. For an instant Wayne was certain he was going to cry. He perched on a stool close to his easel and stared at the painting. As far as Wayne could gather it was meant to be a muscleman emerging from an egg-shell.

'She was murdered, Mr. Wayne,' Ypson said heavily.

'She was murdered. You can call me Joe. Do you have any ideas about it, Harold?'

Ypson made a negative gesture. He moved his head sideways slightly, lifted his right hand slightly. Wayne wondered if he thought entirely by symbols.

'When did you see her last, Harold?' he said.

'A week ago. Ten days ago. I'm not sure

really. I had a crush on her. I used to go to the club where she worked and listen to her singing. She had the most wonderful voice, Mr. Wayne.'

'I'll take your word for it. Were you in love with her, Harold?'

Ypson swivelled to face Wayne now. A crooked smile creased grooves at his mouth.

'Not really. Oh, I liked Mitzi, Mr. Wayne, but I was smart enough to know where to stop.'

Wayne frowned. He was going off Ypson of a sudden.

'What are you trying to say, pal?'

Ypson closed his eyes momentarily. He seemed to have trouble making up his mind about something. His features sobered.

'If you don't already know, Mr. Wayne, Mitzi was too fond of men ever to settle down with any one of them.'

'That's not a very nice thing to say about somebody who isn't around to defend herself.'

Ypson shrugged. It was almost a careless gesture.

'You want to hear what I know. You want to hear what I think. Mitzi is dead. I'm terribly sorry she's dead. She was murdered. I have an idea why she was murdered.'

'You get more illuminating by the minute,' Wayne said drily. 'At first I figured you were scared out of your underwear. But don't let my comments inhibit you. Go on.'

'Jealousy,' Ypson announced dramatically. 'What other reason could there be, Mr. Wayne? She must have been stringing somebody along; obviously she was stringing somebody along. Then she gives her favours to somebody else, and — Need I say any more, Mr. Wayne?'

'You've said plenty.'

Wayne came to his feet. He felt like punching Harold Ypson on his handsome nose. He was annoyed at the interview turning out this way. He had come here expecting to find someone pining for a hopeless cause. All he had found was an artist who was about three-quarters crazy. He knew what was really troubling him, though. He had hoped for a real break from Ypson. He had got something to be sure, but it didn't fit in with the rest of the picture.

'Would you care for a cup of coffee before you go, Mr. Wayne?'

'No, thanks. I wouldn't like to keep you from having your long walk. Did you know that Mitzi ran her own car?'

'The one she was killed in? Yes. I can't get it out of my mind. Do you think the police will be calling to see me too, Mr. Wayne?'

'It's possible. Goodbye, Harold.'

'Just a minute, Mr. Wayne . . . '

'Yeah?' Wayne faced him again and waited.

'There is one thing that might shed some light on the affair. I noticed that Mitzi usually had a large sum of money in her purse.'

Wayne's eyes narrowed. 'You saw it when you searched?'

'I didn't have to search. I just saw it. And that car. It must have set her back more dough than she ever earned singing in the clubs.'

'I don't know what I'd have done

without you, Harold. Anything else while you're in an expansive mood?'

Ypson began to colour.

'You remind me of that bastard at the agency,' he said. 'I don't mind if the police do call.'

Wayne left him while he was still in control of himself.

★   ★   ★

Hank Petersen was chatting with Maggie Yarmon when Wayne returned to his office. Just then Petersen was one of the last people Wayne wished to talk to. He knew by the glint in the cop's eye that something was on his mind.

'Miss Yarmon was telling me how you're making like a little eager beaver, Joe.'

'You're kidding.'

A furtive glance at Maggie brought a furtive wink in turn. Maggie Yarmon had been around Wayne for long enough to learn what bluff was.

'He tries to feel my leg again, I'll scream, Joe. You'd better leave me a gun behind when you go out.'

'Don't push it, sweetheart,' Petersen told her. 'If you do I'll come and haunt you some dark night. I've got a chain hasn't been clanked in a long time. I want a word with you, Joe,' he added to Wayne. 'Anybody holed up in the back office?'

'It's not a very good way to catch a killer, Hank.'

'It won't take long. Come on, pal.'

In the rear office Petersen closed the door behind them and slumped on a chair. He lifted a bronze paper-weight and examined it closely.

'Who were the two mutts, Joe?'

'You're talking about last night, Hank?'

'I'm talking about last night,' Petersen said. 'A certain dame figured she ought to make a clean breast of everything before she's found in a car that's only running on three wheels.'

It sounded like Sally Rogan to Wayne. The girl was getting nervous about the whole business. At least it showed she was really nothing more than an innocent bystander.

'A dame called Sally?' he said to Petersen.

'You saw her at the Jackpot Club. You made a date to take her home. She says you got some kind of message that sent you home ahead of her. Two guys were waiting to pass the time of day. Is that what happened up to there, Joe?'

'That's it, Hank,' Wayne said slowly. He wondered if he should level with Petersen all the way, tell him about following the toughs and where they had ended up. He didn't see much sense in holding it back.

Petersen was thoughtful when he had finished talking. He placed the paperweight on the desk and scratched his jaw.

'That's where Cotter's brother hangs out,' he said finally.

'I had Maggie check the address. We found out the resident was called Cotter. I didn't know what connection he had with Morton. So he's got a brother. Apparently he doesn't like me. Apparently too, Morton doesn't go for me much. It's enough to make a guy take a long look at his ego, Hank.'

'It ought to be enough to encourage

you to drop your client and find a new one, Joe,' Petersen said soberly.

'Just when I'm getting warm? Come off it, Hank. We've got enough evidence as it is to bring both Cotter boys in on suspicion.'

'Of what?' Petersen murmured. 'Having a strong dislike for private eyes? You must be nuts. Okay. So you didn't get a hearty welcome at *Greenmere*. You met two punks at the dame's place who roughed you around. Do you think Cotter's brother is going to admit he sent them to rough you around?'

'But Sally Rogan's evidence — '

'Hold it right there, bub. We've had one girl smashed up in a car. We don't want another one until we solve the first case. Is it all right with you, Joe?'

'But you think I'm onto something good, Hank?'

'Could be you are. Could be you're following nothing but a red herring.'

'Great! And what do you want me to do — hide my light somewhere while you and the police department grab the medals?'

'What I want you to do is go easy, Joe,' Petersen amended soberly. 'Don't raise any smoke. Don't scare potential witnesses before we're ready to grab them.' Petersen got up and went to the door. He had a thin smile on his face. 'As a matter of fact, Joe, I think you're a pretty smart cookie. But easy does it, huh?'

'You wouldn't be protecting the Cotters, Hank?'

'I ought to spit in your eye for that one, pal. I'm just saying easy does it. Don't queer the pitch.'

'Okay. So long as you don't bust any stitches.'

It was another time when Wayne suspected he was being manipulated by somebody. He hated being manipulated by the cops.

11

The rest of the day was comparatively colourless. Wayne had a visit from Dell Lavers around noon. Lavers fancied he should have come up with something concrete by this time. He was disappointed and cut up when Wayne told him he had made a little progress, but not much, and that Lavers would be doing him a big service if he stayed off his back.

'Give me a break for a couple of days,' he said to Lavers. 'I've been told by a very knowledgeable guy to take it easy. I haven't had much experience in murder, you know.'

'Take it easy!' Lavers ejaculated. 'A couple of days . . . Why, in a couple more days this killer will have covered his tracks effectively. What do you propose to do then?'

'I'll keep on the ball until you say to come off it, Dell,' Wayne told him. 'In the meantime you have the comforting thought that the police are leaving no stone unturned.'

'The police!' Lavers snarled. 'Oh yeah! This is just too hilarious for words. No stone unturned! I've the feeling I've heard that one before somewhere as well.'

There and then Wayne had given Lavers an ultimatum. Either he backed off and was patient or he could go out and find himself another private operator.

Lavers departed on that note. When he had gone Maggie Yarmon thought that Wayne had treated him more harshly than was necessary.

'After all, Joe, you've got to see his view-point too. It was his sister was killed. It was his sister was going to have somebody's baby.'

Maggie didn't have to remind him. Find the man Mitzi Laverick was in love with, he thought. Find the man that Mitzi had grown afraid of and was trying to escape. They must be the same man. They just had to be the same man. Only, if the girl had been in love with the man, why did she feel it necessary to get away from him? Why couldn't they have settled the problem in a civilised fashion?

Of course there was another side to the shabby and tragic picture. Mitzi Laverick may not have been in love with anyone. If half of what Harold Ypson had told him was true, it meant that Mitzi had bestowed her favours with a spendthrift's disregard for the day after tomorrow.

In the early afternoon he had a call from Dave Chalmers of the *Herald*. The general tone of Chalmer's communication was of impatience tempered with puzzlement.

'I figured you'd have the whole thing sewed up and delivered by this time, Joe,' he said. 'Are you taking a back seat after they nearly killed you too?'

'I'm wearing my brains out, if you want to know, Dave. I might have a lead; I can't be sure till I check and double check. The girl's brother wants me to stay with it.'

'What do you think of the girl's brother, Joe?'

'Nothing in particular. Just now he's making himself a pain in my neck. It's understandable in view of the situation.'

'He knows his sister was pregnant?'

'He does. You've kept that out of the reports, Dave. Is it on account of squeamishness in your old age?'

'Not so you'd notice. The cops figured the angle. I'm not so sure of the wisdom of it, though. Nothing gets the public up in arms like a good sob story. If they heard the facts they might come from all corners with information.'

'It's two-sided too, Dave. It opens the door for cranks, do-gooders and nuts who want to confess to all the sins in the world.'

'Okay, Joe. Good luck. Think of me if it breaks. Be hearing from you.'

Wayne had a sudden thought. 'Hold on, Dave. The dame worked at one of Mort Cotter's clubs — '

'I know. She had a kind of rep too, if you haven't heard.'

Wayne frowned. 'Gossip always find a way, huh?'

'That's right. But what's with Cotter?'

'He's got a brother in town. Did you know that?'

'Frank? Yeah. He helps Mort run those

outfits. What's on your mind, Joe?'

Wayne's hesitation was brief. He knew he could trust Chalmers to be cautious and discreet.

'If you could get some info on Frank, Dave; the circles he moves in.'

'I'll try. Anything for a pal. Goodbye, Joe.'

★   ★   ★

In the evening Wayne was tempted to call at Frank Cotter's place on Huxley Park. He had a good reason for making a visit if he cared to use it. He would explain about Charley and his scar-faced friend, and ask Cotter pointblank if he had ordered the men to beat him up.

He decided against this course. The best he could hope for was a sample of the cold-shoulder treatment that Mort had dished out; the worst could be a flat denial of his charges. The wise thing to do was wait for Morton Cotter or his brother to make the next move towards him.

According to the reactions he had drawn from both members of the Cotter family, they knew more about Mitzi Laverick's murder than anybody else he could think of. But, as Hank Petersen had made clear, those same reactions could not be construed as positive evidence of guilt, or even involvement with the slayer of the girl.

Also, there was just the chance that Morton Cotter's brush-off at *Greenmere*, and the fracas with the pair who had waited for him at Sally Rogan's apartment, were cunning manoeuvres to make a smoke-screen for the purpose of putting both him and the police on a false trail.

By morning he had formulated a revised plan of approach to the problem.

The police were in possession of the murder car, and he drove to Cressley Street to ask if he could look at it.

'You sure you've brought your magnifying glass along, Mr. Wayne?' was the crack that greeted him from the sergeant in charge of the general office.

'I just want another look. I promise not to take away more than a wing for a souvenir.'

'In that case go ahead. You know where

we keep stuff like that?'

'I know.'

The car was on a private area at the rear of the headquarters building. An officer escorted him through a gate and stood off while Wayne went over to the vehicle. A lot of car dealers put an advertising sticker on the models they sold. There was one on the Dodge. The car had been bought from Heathcroft Motors. Wayne pretended to look around for the benefit of the watching cop. He lit a cigarette finally and went back to the gate.

'There's no doubt that the studs were filed,' the cop said on his way out with him. 'But the guy who wanted it to look like an accident must have been crazy.'

'How come?' Wayne asked curiously. The cop was young and bright, and might have heard things that hadn't reached his ears.

'Easy. He was crazy if he thought the filed studs wouldn't be noticed when the car was found.'

'You make a good point. But how do you know the killer didn't bank on the heap going up in flames? It's what usually happens in a crash of this sort. If it had happened, I wouldn't be standing here talking to you.'

The cop grinned. 'You make a good point yourself, Mr. Wayne. But nowadays we always go over accident vehicles with the greatest care.'

'I should have thought of that. Thanks for the help.'

Wayne mulled it over as he drove across town. What the cop said could be true enough, but there were fires and fires, and a good one would give the police plenty to do to salvage a reason for the crash.

He had thought he knew where Heathcroft Motors was located, but when he stopped on Colfax he realised he had the wrong name in mind. The place he was looking at was called Hetheringtons. He cruised to a drugstore and went through the telephone book. Heathcroft Motors was on Lawrence Street at the opposite side of town.

He arrived at the place and walked into the reception office to ask for the manager. The manager was busy with a customer, he was told. He could see him in five or ten minutes if he cared to wait. He spotted the manager with the customer, but according to the line the manager was giving a fat man who smoked a cigar, he was only a potential customer at the moment.

Wayne spent the time in having a look at the latest models on display. There was no harm in looking, he thought. He would have to get another year at least out of the Plymouth.

Eventually the manager, whose name was Rawlins, was through and came over to him.

'Good morning, sir! Thinking of something fresh and racy?'

'I'm sorry to disappoint you. No, as a matter of fact I'm thinking of something that's waiting for the junkyard man to call.'

The man's mouth was sagging when Wayne flashed his photostat. He gathered himself and brought his smile back again. It was feeble and mildly apprehensive.

'A private detective. I see! But what can I do to help you?'

'I'm inquiring about a Dodge was bought here recently, Mr. Rawlins. A two-tone, brown and cream job. As far as I know a girl made the purchase.'

'Of course! I know. The car that Miss Laverick bought from us. Have the police made any headway, did you hear?'

'The police have been with you?' Wayne countered.

'Yes. A man checked to make sure we'd sold the car to Miss Laverick. We arranged for one of our top men to examine the car and compare his findings with those of the police. By the way — ' Rawlins went on. ' — would you be the detective who was travelling with the girl when she crashed?'

Wayne nodded. Rawlins asked him to step into his private office. He offered Wayne a cigarette and regarded him with curious eyes.

'It must have been quite a shock for you. I mean — you could have been killed in the crash too, just as easily as the girl.'

Wayne nodded again. His grin was faint but tolerant. Rawlins struck him like a man who figured he was smarter than most. He was gathering material for the story he would tell his wife or girl-friend over dinner that evening. He wore glasses and took them off to wipe moisture from his left eye.

'The wheel studs were filed,' he went on as he held a lighter for Wayne's cigarette. 'It must have taken some filing to get through those studs.'

'Nobody's blaming anybody in connection with the car, Mr. Rawlins. It'll be a headache for the insurance people. I guess. I don't represent an insurance company however. I represent my client, who is the dead girl's brother.'

'How terrible for him! But the police are busy on the hunt for the murderer — '

'The police are busy on the hunt for the murderer,' Wayne agreed. 'The purpose of my call, Mr. Rawlins — '

'It's a miracle you came out of it alive,' Rawlins gushed. He leaned back on his chair and crossed one leg over the other. He had never been in a situation quite like this. 'But yes! The reason for your call . . . Ha, ha. I was forgetting. You must lead an exciting life indeed, Mr. Wayne.'

'At the moment it's dull enough,' Wayne told him. If Rawlins read the hint he gave no sign. He assured Wayne that he would do everything he could for him, of course. Within reason, of course, if Wayne understood what he meant.

'Of course. I'd like to know when the purchase was made? You do keep records?'

'Ahem! Yes. We're meticulous with regard to records here, Mr. Wayne. Would you stay there while I consult with Miss Baynes in the record office?'

'Thank you.'

Wayne followed Rawlins's progress to the other office through the glass partition. There was also a glass partition in the wall of the records office, and by moving his chair two feet he could have an ample view of what the manager was up to. He didn't quite trust Rawlins. He talked too much, for a start. For another thing, he evinced too strong a curiosity for Wayne's liking.

A typist lifted her head when Rawlins spoke to her. When she squinted at the compartment where Wayne sat he shifted his eyes and pretended to look out at the cars. The next time Wayne glanced at her she was dialling a number on the phone. Rawlins was going through a drawer in what could have been a filing cabinet.

He broke off searching when the secretary held the telephone receiver to him. He turned his back towards Wayne while he talked into it. A few minutes later he found what he wanted in the filing cabinet and left the records office. A man in white overalls who was polishing a car spoke to him. Rawlins said something in reply and entered the office. His face was beaming benevolently.

'Here we are, Mr. Wayne. I hope I didn't keep you too long. I had a little trouble locating the records I needed.'

'Are you sure it's okay to go ahead?'

Rawlins was spreading a ledger on the desk and turned with his mouth sagging again. A flush of colour entered his cheeks.

'I don't understand, Mr. Wayne . . . '

'You were on with the cops just then, I gathered?'

'What a — Really, Mr. Wayne, I — '

'It's all right. Don't swallow your pride in case it chokes you. Who did you get in touch with — Sergeant Petersen?'

Rawlins blinked rapidly behind his glasses. He took them off to wipe moisture from his eye. He tried to laugh but nothing came out but a dry croak.

'You must forgive me, but — '

'Forgiven. Who was it — Petersen?'

'No. As a matter of fact I was speaking with Lieutenant Eckert. In my business I've got to be very careful, Mr. Wayne. Especially now, after what happened to the girl.'

'Eckert said to humour me?'

'He said you were quite trustworthy, if you want to know. He said it was all right to talk with you and give you any information you asked for.'

'It must be my honest face. Okay, pal, there's no harm done. Can you give me some answers now?'

Rawlins took his chair but kept his gaze riveted to his ledger. The blush had crept to his neck and was still spreading.

'Miss Laverick bought the car a month

ago, almost to the day,' he said tonelessly.

'She made the purchase herself?'

'She did. I recalled her when the police came. One of my salesmen was making the deal. He called me in when the sale was finalised.'

'You remember what she looked like?'

'Yes, I do. She had red hair. She — she was a very good-looking girl. Her signature is here if you'd like to check.'

Wayne did. The handwriting was the same as that on the slip of paper he had taken from Mitzi Laverick's handbag.

'So far, so good, Mr. Rawlins. I'm sure I'm just going over ground that the police have covered.'

Rawlins made no attempt to enlighten him. He was closing the ledger when Wayne asked another question.

'How did Miss Laverick pay for the car? Did she take out an H.P. agreement?'

'She paid in cash,' Rawlins said with a touch of curtness. 'Strange as it may seem, we do have the occasional customer who can pay in cash.'

'I wouldn't dream of doubting you. But you're sure she paid by cash and not with a cheque?'

'There's no question about it,' Rawlins said stiffly. 'Here is the entry for the date of purchase.'

Wayne made a mental note of the date of purchase. He rose to his feet, thanked Rawlins warmly and extended his hand.

'You've been a big help.'

Rawlins hesitated over shaking hands. He let Wayne out and said goodbye. He had a pained look in his eye as he watched the Plymouth pull into the traffic.

★   ★   ★

Joe Wayne stopped off at a bar in midtown. He drank a beer and reviewed what he had found out so far about Mitzi Laverick. The purchase of the Dodge by cash was a revelation. But she had bought the car a month ago, so she hadn't bought it with the idea of heading off for anywhere in a hurry. A month ago everything must have been going fine for Mitzi. A month ago she was working at the Jackpot Club, and maybe thinking of the wedding bells that would be ringing in the near future.

Why had the atmosphere changed since then? Why had her lover decided to kill her in preference to marrying her?

Could it be that he was still rushing his fences, and that some vital clue was as yet uncovered? Was he concentrating too intensely on the obvious while some other factor of significance eluded him?

He went into the phone booth and rang Maggie Yarmon. Before Maggie could get going with her cracks he asked her to compile a list of the banks in Darton City.

'I think I know most of them, Maggie, but I want to be sure I don't skip one of them.'

'What's with banks, Joey?' Maggie retorted in mock alarm. 'You start breaking into them and you'll not get past the first teller before they put a ball on your leg. Have second thoughts, Joey, please. If not for your sake, then think of the slur I'll earn. Secretary to a bank-robber! I'd never get another job in ninety-nine years, which is what you'll rate for sure.'

'Knock it off, baby, and do what I say. Call this number when you're ready.' He gave her the booth number and went to the counter for another beer.

He could have checked it out for himself, he thought while he drank the beer. He wondered if he was growing lazy. He wondered if the private eye racket hadn't started to go sour on him. Too many dead dames would turn anything sour.

When the phone rang he hurried back to the booth.

12

It was a long job he had set himself; it didn't make him the most popular person with the bank managers he talked with. He struck oil after his fourth call. The fifth bank on his list was Merchants and Western Consolidated. The manager was a thin, anaemic man who kept staring at Wayne's tie as though it was some rare curio. He didn't care to discuss his customers' accounts, was his opening line. There were some exceptions to the rule, of course, but Wayne could see that he was going to have great difficulty in finding one.

Even his licence left the manager cold.

'But you did have a customer named Mitzi Laverick,' he pressed. 'You've admitted as much.'

'Admit is an unfortunate word in this context, Mr. Wayne,' he was sternly reminded. 'And I'm afraid you'll have to be more persuasive than you have been this far.'

'I could offer you a lump of sugar.'

'Being facetious will get you nowhere,' was the prim response. 'And now if you'll — '

'All right, Mr. Milner, I see that you haven't heard the news about Miss Laverick. Miss Laverick is dead. She had an accident. Her car was involved in a crash. Her brother has retained me to look into certain aspects of her background. Would that sort of persuasion get me anywhere, do you think?'

It seemed it would. Milner called for books and took Wayne to his private cubby hole. Another revelation was sprung on Wayne. Over a period of three months Mitzi Laverick had deposited money to the amount of twenty-five thousand dollars.

'How did she pay the money into her account?' he asked when he had weathered the shock. 'Pay-cheque, I guess?'

It turned out his guess was wrong; it turned out that Mitzi had made her deposits in cash. One deposit alone was for ten thousand dollars. This was the initial one. The next deposit had been five thousand dollars in cash. The last one had been made two weeks ago — five thousand dollars in cash.

Wayne lit a cigarette to hide his feelings. He grinned at Milner.

'There was one dame knew how to make money. I wish somebody would give me a couple of secrets.'

'How a customer earns the cash he deposits is no concern of ours, Mr. Wayne. By the way, the lady was not mixed up in anything crooked, I hope?'

'Not a chance,' Wayne said quickly. The last thing he wanted now was for Milner to get in touch with the police. This could be the lead he was searching for, and if the police took a too close interest it might complicate matters. 'The girl was a marvellous singer,' he added. 'Singers don't get paid in peanuts these days, you know.'

'I know.' Milner shuddered. 'Personally I fail to appreciate the value of this so-called pop music.'

'You and me, Mr. Milner. One thing

more, if you don't mind — did Miss Laverick make any substantial withdrawals during the last day or so?'

A faint smile flitted over the other's pale face. 'I was wondering if you'd ask me that question. Yes, she did. She drew every last red cent four days ago.'

This time Wayne couldn't quite control his features. His eyes widened and his jaw dropped.

'In cash?'

'In cash, Mr. Wayne. I did think it rather unusual. I remember I asked her if she was thinking of leaving town. It was a stupid question, of course — but — well, I was mildly curious. I take a certain interest in our customers, you know.'

Wayne said, 'I see.' He stood up and offered Milner his hand. 'You've been very helpful. Now I'll be able to give her brother the news, and be able to brag about a satisfied customer myself. Goodday to you, Mr. Milner.'

'Goodday to you,' Milner said as he gathered up his books. He didn't look at Wayne on his way to the street.

Wayne went into a pay-phone and rang his office again.

'Listen, Maggie,' he said, 'something has cropped up. I'm going to take a drive and may not come back tonight. Any calls come in, you can make a note of them.'

'But what if there happens to be something urgent, Joey? And where are you heading for anyhow?'

'Ashbury,' Wayne told her. 'I think I started off on this case with the wrong foot. Maybe I'm getting into stride now. The dame had twenty-five thousand bucks deposited at the Merchants and Western Consolidated.'

'Mitzi — '

'That's right,' Wayne broke in on Maggie. 'So what do you think of it now, baby?'

'She must have had a swell voice,' Maggie said drily.

'I figured you'd say something of the sort, honey. But you don't really mean it, do you?'

'Grow up, Joe. Look — ' She dropped her voice. ' — this could be the reason for the — uh — accident, Joe. I mean, if she had an accident she could hardly deposit any more large sums of money. And the guy who was paying the money — '

'Let it drift, Maggie. And not a word to anyone about it. Where will you be this evening?'

'You want me to go along as body-guard?'

'I don't,' Wayne said. 'But if you happened to be at your own little shack out on Nash Street . . . '

'So I would be handy if you want to make a call? Well, okay, Joey. I wouldn't do it for everybody, mind you. Look, make it a date and ring me around nine. That suit?'

'You're a treasure, Maggie. It might not be necessary, but it'll cut both ways as you can give me any dope that happens between now and then.'

'There was another call from you-know-who. I almost forgot in the excitement.'

'Dell?'

'Yeah. He's a nice guy, but I wish somebody would ban him for about a year. All he can say is how are you getting on . . . Joe! You don't think that Dell and his sister were running a duet on some guy? The inspiration just hit me.'

'It's a thought, Maggie. I'll mull it over. See you.'

As Wayne stepped out of the phone booth he happened to be looking straight in front of him. A delivery truck was parked at the kerb; a car was parked behind it. The man at the wheel of the car turned his head away suddenly as Wayne's gaze touched him. Wayne looked at the man again. He was dark-featured, and the eyes that had locked briefly with his own were sloe-black.

Wayne walked on past and halted casually at a newsstand. He bought a paper and pretended to scan the front page. The car with the dark-featured man was on the move and edging into the traffic.

Something alarmed in Wayne's memory. Lashlin, the motorcycle cop had told him of a dark-skinned man halting at the bend in the Ashbury road. He shrugged and went to his own car. He lit a cigarette before opening up and getting under the wheel. There was no sign of the other car as he drove off.

Clear of Darton City he cruised at a steady fifty until he reached the bad bend. At this stage more memories came back to him. Of Mitzi Laverick at his side in her Dodge. Her nearness had been like a drug to him, he recalled. He had just been asking her what she was running away from. He had asked her a dozen times before. The answer was always the same. Please forget it, she said. He was being paid, she said. It was all he needed to be concerned about.

The fence at the bend had been repaired and he glanced at the rocks beyond on his way past. A cold sweat broke on his brow when he thought of what could have happened to him in there.

The road to Ashbury was anything but a good one and he didn't push the Plymouth. Arriving, he found a small hotel and left his car on the parking area at the rear. He freshened up and ate lunch. In the lobby, with a cigarette burning, he shut himself in a phone booth and took out ballpen and notepad. By the time he had culled the information he needed it was too late to go on a bank crawl.

He booked a room at the hotel and went up to lie down for an hour. He wondered why Mitzi Laverick had picked on this town to come to. Did she have a contact in Ashbury that she wished to meet, or had she simply chosen the place at random as a whistle stop on her journey to elsewhere?

Wayne was lying on the bed covers when the phone rang. He sat up and stubbed his cigarette out on a tray. Then he ran a hand across his head and made wild guesses. It might only be the desk clerk wanting to check on something, he decided. But this wasn't the sort of hotel where the desk clerks worried about the backgrounds of their roomers.

He lifted the phone finally and said hello.

'Mr. Wayne?' It was the desk clerk's voice he was sure. He knew a wave of relief.

'What is it?'

'A gentleman wishes to speak with you. Can I put him on?'

'Why not?' Wayne said after an instant's hesitation.

Another voice spoke in his ear almost immediately. It was a voice that was entirely new to Wayne.

'Hello there, Mr. Wayne. Sorry to trouble you like this, but I'd like to have a word with you.'

Wayne said coolly, 'Help yourself. It's not costing me anything.' His mind raced frantically, trying to pin down somebody who could have tailed him here to Ashbury. He thought of the dark-skinned man and his mouth tightened.

'I'd much rather talk to you in private,' came the equally cool response.

'I see. What reasons do you have? I'm a stranger to town. At least I thought I was a stranger to town. I've only just arrived here anyhow. I happen to be enjoying a short vacation. How's about finding yourself somebody else to talk to?'

A short laugh answered him.

'I really think you should see me, Mr. Wayne. I won't take up much of your time. Perhaps I might even make your vacation a more pleasant one.'

'Now you've hooked me, pal. Okay. Come right up.'

He put the phone back on its hook, slid out the .38 from its sheath. He returned the gun to the holster almost immediately and opened the door an inch.

Three minutes later he heard footsteps in the passage.

The footsteps were light and unhurried. They halted at the door and knuckles rapped sharply.

'Mr. Wayne . . . '

'It's open.'

The door was pushed ajar and the dark-skinned man with the black eyes eased into the room. He had a Colt automatic in his right hand and gestured with it while he closed the room door with a heel.

'Please sit down, Mr. Wayne.'

Wayne stood where he was. He snapped, 'Who are you? What's the big idea? Who's teaching you all these bad habits?'

The man smiled faintly. Wayne noticed

that the smile curled the corners of his narrow mouth slightly; it didn't travel as far as the black eyes. The eyes remained flat and cold and repulsive. They reminded Wayne of a snake's.

'One thing at a time,' he said conversationally. 'First of all I'd like you to take that chair.'

'First of all you'd better explain yourself, sonny,' Wayne growled. 'And it better be real good or I'll be tempted to kick you twice in the pants.'

'So you won't listen to reason.'

There was regret in the man's voice now. It wasn't showing anywhere else that Wayne could notice. He took a slow step to the chair being indicated and sank down onto the edge of it.

'That's much better!'

'You only think it is, chum. From here I can get a real good kick at something else before I start in on your pants.'

The smile dwindled from the narrow lips and left them flat and bleak as his eyes. He made another gesture with the gun.

'Put your hands on the top of your

head. Come on! I'm not going to spend all day listening to your cheap gags.'

Wayne saw that delaying tactics were out; he saw too that he had been a fool to put his .38 back in its holster. When he crooked his arms to place his hands on the crown of his head his coat fell open to reveal the shoulder harness and the weapon it contained.

The stranger lifted the gun clear swiftly and expertly. He laid it down on the table by the door that held the phone.

'Have you got any other playthings on you?'

'Yeah. A dagger in my belt and a blowpipe down my sock. Can we cut the comedy and get down to business?'

'I guess we can.'

The man lifted the other chair in the room and placed it with its back against the door. Then he sat down on the chair and rested the gun on his lap while he flipped a cigarette from a pocket and lit it with a lighter.

'I saw that trick in a movie,' Wayne said. 'The guy put his gun down the way you've done. But the guy he was holding up made a charge at him. The guy grabbed his gun right enough. He used it too. But you know who he shot?'

'Knock it off,' was the crisp admonition. The man lifted his gun again. 'I want to talk business with you, Mr. Wayne. I hope you'll agree with the proposal I have to make.'

'Is it your proposal or is somebody writing your script?'

'That's neither here nor there. The point is that I'm handling the situation. You went round a lot of banks in Darton City this morning. Why did you do that?'

'I like banks. I'm very fond of banks. I put a few bucks in one one time. I couldn't remember which one it was. So I went round each of them to find out.'

Annoyance crept into the eyes of the dark man.

'So you're going to be tedious. It won't do, you know. I'm not playing games with you.'

'I'm glad to hear it. Last game you played where I was involved I got a very sore head out of it. I don't go for playing games with guys like you, pal. You might as well get that under your toupee for a start. Call it being a cautious so-and-so. Call it anything you fancy. Just count me out.'

'You found what you wanted at the Merchants and Western, Mr. Wayne. You discovered that Mitzi Laverick had an account there.'

He paused for Wayne to comment. Wayne picked a spot in the centre of the man's forehead and stared at it. He didn't say anything.

'Okay, Wayne! Be stubborn if you want to. But here's what I'm getting at. I've got news for you. Not good news, I'm afraid, unless you're sensible enough to want to go on living.'

'Now you pain me, pal. On the phone you said you could make my vacation a more pleasant one. All you've done this far is put me off guys with sallow faces and black eyes for ever.'

The stranger sneered at him.

'Anything can be more pleasant if you're alive to enjoy it. If you happen to be dead you don't get much of a fling any more.'

'You're real bright for a sucker. Just how big a sucker are you? Haven't you ever heard of the facts of life? Haven't you ever learned what happens to mugs who go around killing people? Did somebody tell you to kill me?'

'That's beside the point.'

'It's a good point all the same. Okay, pal, get it off your chest. You've been hired by the meanie who filed the studs on Mitzi Laverick's car. Maybe you even did that little job by your own cute self. Maybe you had high hopes of me getting my come-uppance in the crash too. So you've got the drop on me. So that's fine. So where do we go from here?'

'What are you doing in Ashbury?' the visitor said softly. He had finished with his cigarette and killed it by placing it on the floor and using his heel.

'Like I told you before you scared the daylights out of me — taking a vacation.'

'You're a liar, Wayne. The girl's brother hired you to snoop around. You got permission from the cops to snoop around. I'm telling you to stop the snooping. I'm telling you to get into your heap and head for home.'

'Telling isn't the same thing as coaxing, chum.'

The man's sneer widened.

'You're angling for a hand-out? You've got as much chance as I have of flying. No handouts. No bribery. Just a plain old-fashioned warning to take your nose the hell out of the soup or be killed in the line of duty.'

'Then you didn't come up here to kill me?'

'I don't want to kill you, shamus. I don't go in for killing if it can be avoided. I'm giving you your chance.'

'Did you give Mitzi Laverick her chance too, or has the generous mood just taken you?'

The man was silent for a moment, then he said flatly, 'The dame had her chance. She wouldn't grab it.'

'Now you begin to interest me. Tell me more. If I was to hear the right way of the thing I might even come down on your side.'

'I'm sorry.'

The man rose to his feet and moved the

chair aside. He pointed the gun at Wayne's chest while his black eyes glittered.

'Don't make me do it, Mr. Wayne. Don't make me do it.'

With that he opened the door and backed into the passage. Wayne grabbed his gun and went after him. He saw the man race past the elevator to reach the stairway. When Wayne arrived at the stairway there was no sign of the other.

He hurried down all the same and came to a halt in the lobby. The desk clerk lifted his head to stare at him.

'Is something the matter, Mr. Wayne?'

'My friend forgot something. Has he gone out yet?'

'Right this minute. If you make it fast . . . '

Wayne did make it fast. He hit the sidewalk as a car drew into the traffic and roared off. In another minute it had gained the end of the street and vanished from sight.

13

For the next hour Wayne searched for the car and the dark-featured man who was driving it. The car was a Ford, a grey coupé which would be readily recognisable if he saw it again. He hadn't managed to get the licence number.

He knew Ashbury pretty well and looked in all the likely spots; it was impossible however to cover the whole town, and the stranger could have gone back to Darton City straightaway, when he had performed his frightening-off act. Wayne didn't think he had returned to Darton City, though. If he was so interested in the activities of the investigator, he would hang around Ashbury to find out what he was up to.

Wayne wasn't sure that he knew what he was up to himself. So far he had been moving about mostly in the dark. His discovery of Mitzi Laverick's banking account had provided a lead of sorts, a lead which he intended following up in the morning. It might take him nowhere, of course; on the other hand some clue might emerge that could provide a definite pointer.

Back at the hotel he locked the door of his room and went over the problem step by step. Mitzi Laverick had called on his services because she was scared, and in the light of subsequent events the girl had every reason to be scared. She had wished to get out of Darton City and come to Ashbury. Why Ashbury? Wayne wondered. Why couldn't she have chosen some other town? Why, if she wished to escape whatever danger was dogging her, didn't she travel as far away from Darton City as possible?

It might have been the girl's intention. As had suggested itself to Wayne before, Ashbury might simply have been the first stepping stone on a much longer journey. There was the other side of the coin too. Once in Ashbury the girl might have considered herself safe. Other protection might have taken over here. But what sort of protection, and provided by whom?

It seemed clear to Wayne that Morton Cotter was somehow involved with the tragedy of Mitzi Laverick, his brother Frank too. If this wasn't so then why the necessity to persuade him to mind his own business? Why the need to put the dark-featured man on his trail?

Other questions clamoured in Wayne's mind and mingled with a host of speculations. In the end the whole problem appeared to revolve on one pivot — the man who had been the club singer's lover. But if there had been a lot of lovers, as Harold Ypson had intimated . . . He gave up puzzling at that juncture.

At nine o'clock Wayne rang Maggie Yarmon's home number on Nash Street in Darton City. Maggie replied at once and asked how things were going.

'Not too well, I'm afraid, Maggie. I did have a visit from a guy who warned me to lay off. I tried to follow him, but he was moving too fast and gave me the slip.'

'Cotter has put him onto you, Joey. I just know that Cotter is behind the whole set-up. You're nuts if you don't see it. The cops are nuts if they don't see it. And speaking of cops, Joe, there was a phone call from Hank Petersen just after you rang me to say you were going to Ashbury.'

'What did Hank want?'

'What do you think? Information. He's got the whole murder squad working at the thing and he asks a guy like you for information! Oh, I'm not saying you're not a swell operator, Joe. But it's all so simple to me it makes me gnash my teeth. Look — the dame — Mitzi, I mean — was working for Cotter. You find she's been stashing away large sums of dough. That spells blackmail to me with a capital B. She was playing around with Cotter. She finds she's going to have a baby. When Morton hears he nearly flips . . . '

'So you think he began to pay her sums of money to keep her mouth shut?'

'Isn't it what you think yourself, Joey? I understood it's what you thought anyhow.'

'I know. But I've been mulling it over, Maggie. It would have been a lot simpler for Cotter — if her lover was Cotter — to wash his hands of Mitzi and tell her to jump off a bridge if she felt like it. He didn't need to hand her a load of dough. He didn't need hand her anything but a big goodbye.'

Maggie Yarmon was silent for a moment while she thought about that. Then, reluctantly, 'Yeah, I think I see what you're driving at, Joe. So she must have got the dough from somebody else then, which puts us right back where we started.'

'Possibly, Maggie, but not necessarily.'

'Look, Joe, she did or she didn't. Cotter did or he didn't. It's getting a bit too complicated for me, especially at this time of evening when I ought to be out enjoying myself.'

'Yeah. Me too. I'm sorry, baby. Sweet dreams — '

'No! Hold it, Joe. You've got me hooked on this darn thing now and I can't get off it. If Mort Cotter or his brother didn't give Mitzi the dough, then who did?'

'Why ask me, honey? Better ask the guy that arranged for the car crash.'

Maggie made a harsh noise in her throat.

'I think you're getting too smart, buster. You know more about this than you're willing to tell. It's no wonder that Hank Petersen's so keen on you.'

Wayne laughed shortly.

'I wish I did, Maggie. See you tomorrow sometime. I hope. Maybe I'll have an inspiration when I go to bed.'

'That I wouldn't doubt at all, pal. But if this Ruth dame hears about it she'll tear your inspiration's hair out.'

It was the note Wayne hung up on.

★　★　★

When the banks opened in the morning he was at the doorway of the first one on his list. He had a better reception here than at any of the banks in Darton City. It might be the difference in the air, he thought. Ashbury was farther inland than Darton City. He mentioned this to the bank manager when he had flashed his licence and been offered a cigarette. The manager laughed.

'Don't bet all your chips on the air, Mr. Wayne. I've just heard that my daughter's given birth to a boy. I've waited around for a long time to become a granddad. I feel like kissing everybody this morning.'

'I didn't have a good shave,' Wayne grinned. 'You want to kiss me you'll have to kiss me on the forehead, granddad.'

No girl by name of Mitzi Laverick had opened an account at the bank. No girl by any name had opened a new account during the last week.

Wayne shook the manager's hand and left.

The result was the same at the next bank, and the next, and the next.

By noon he had covered all the banks in Ashbury and stopped off at a diner for a steak lunch. It didn't figure somehow: something was out of focus. Mitzi Laverick had been in possession of twenty-five thousand dollars before she left Darton City. She didn't have twenty-five thousand dollars on her person when she was killed in her car. She had five hundred dollars on her person when she was killed in her car. So what had happened to the other twenty-odd thousand?

One possible answer could be that whoever had given the girl the money in the first place had taken the trouble of reclaiming most of it. After all, Mitzi was frightened half to death when she called on him at his office. Cotter, if the culprit was Cotter — either Morton or Frank — could have visited the girl at her apartment and demanded the money again. Threats might have been used to persuade Mitzi to cough up and move on out of Darton City. With this objective in mind, the killer had then arranged for the wheel of the Dodge to be tampered with so that Mitzi would never reach her destination. Exit Mitzi, together with the secret of her lover's identity.

Another solution to the problem of the disappearing twenty-odd thousand occurred to Wayne. The girl hadn't been coming to Ashbury on the blind at all. She knew someone here in town, had planned on staying with someone here in Ashbury. It could be a close friend perhaps — someone to whom she had entrusted the money beforehand. But who?

Wayne was on his second cup of coffee when a man crossed the floor of the diner and took a chair at his table. It was the sallow-skinned man and Wayne rose instinctively to his feet, hands balling into fists.

A cold smile played on him.

'Don't do anything childish, shamus. All you'll have for your trouble is the seat of your pants mussed up on the sidewalk. This is a respectable joint, if you don't know. They don't go for guys who start brawls for no reason.'

Wayne sat down again slowly, his eyes drilling into the other. 'You're quite a little gold-mine of information, pal, aren't you? And don't tell me you've spent the morning making like my shadow's got lost somewhere.'

The man signalled to a waiter and asked for a cup of coffee. 'Maybe my friend would like something else too,' he added with a faint sneer.

Wayne shook his head. He lit a cigarette while the coffee was bought. The man across the table from him drummed with long and slim fingers. Wayne slipped his hand under his coat and palmed the .38. He held it in such a way that it was visible only to the stranger.

'What do you intend to do with it?'

'Shoot about six of your teeth down your throat, chum.'

A careless shrug of shoulders greeted the threat.

'One thing about you private eyes, Mr. Wayne, you develop a nice line of patter. What do you do, though, when you need an ounce of common or garden sense?'

'We weep in somebody's handkerchief.'

'I'd be the last one to doubt it. Here's the waiter. Why don't you put that thing out of sight before he has you arrested?'

Wayne eased the .38 into its sheath. When the waiter went away the stranger reached for his coffee. Wayne stretched his hand out and tipped the coffee into the man's lap.

'You clumsy bastard!' the other hissed. He jerked his chair back and began wiping himself. The waiter came over and stared at him.

'Can I do something for you, sir?'

'Yeah. You can go away and keep your

nose to yourself. I hate nosey guys like hell.'

The waiter retreated and the dark-skinned man drew his chair up to the table again. It was thirty seconds before he recovered his composure.

'That was a kid trick, Wayne,' he said hoarsely.

'So what? You played a kid trick on me yesterday. Now we're evens-stevens. Do you want to continue, or would you rather go off some place and puke?'

'I thought you'd realise what you're up against, Wayne. I thought you'd have enough brains to pack up and get back to your knitting.'

'But who says I'm not knitting, pal? Who says I'm not making something real cute for you to wear?'

'I want you to back off before you have to be killed, mug. Doesn't that get through to you at all?'

'It's making my blood run cold. What is your name anyway — Black-eyed Pete?'

'My name means nothing to you. What should concern you is the danger you're in. You went round the banks in Darton

223

City yesterday. This morning you went round the banks here. What are you trying to find — the dough that Mitzi Laverick owned?'

Wayne's mouth tightened. He had the uneasy feeling that the stranger could have a couple of bolts loose in his head. He had no guarantee that the man mightn't suddenly draw his Colt automatic and start shooting. Something of his thoughts must have been transmitted to the other.

'You think I'm crazy, don't you?'

'Of course I do. The way a fox is crazy. Look, are we going to sit here all day and spit at each other?'

'Have you got any better ideas?' was the cool retort.

'I've got one good one. We could talk. We could make like two civilised and sane citizens. We might even get around to asking each other a little of our different backgrounds. Do you have any objections?'

'Go ahead,' the other said. He was smiling with his teeth. He hadn't been using the toothpaste that brings out the best in a smile. 'I'm a reasonable man,

Wayne. If I wasn't you wouldn't be sitting there right now. You'd have a hole in your head and your toes turned up. But don't run away with the notion that it's too late to get into that condition. It's not.'

'Okay. Here's a simple one for openers. Did Mort Cotter hire you to tail me around?'

'Who's Mort Cotter when he's in circulation?'

'That's not an answer, ugly. That's plain and unadulterated prevarication. If you don't know Morton Cotter, how did you learn about the money that Mitzi Laverick owned?'

'I've got ways and means,' was the somewhat smug response. Once again Wayne had the feeling that he was dealing with a form of maniac. And if the stranger didn't know Morton Cotter, and wasn't working for Morton Cotter, just where did he fit into the scheme of things?

'Let's put it another way,' Wayne suggested. 'For the sake of your argument we'll say you don't know Morton Cotter. Do you know his brother, Frank?'

'Look, Wayne, you're doing nothing but

twisting your brains in knots. What I know and whom I know is my own business. Your sort of questions are futile and irrelevant to the real issue.'

'Which is?' Wayne urged.

'You're meddling with something that doesn't concern you. The way you — '

'But it does concern me,' Wayne broke in sharply. 'The girl's brother hired me to find out who had it in for her. That gives me all the reason I need for meddling to my heart's content. If you think I'm at loggerheads with the cops, you're nuts. The cops and I get along fine. In fact I've got a bright idea about now that I could do worse than hand you over to the cops.'

'You wouldn't! What would you tell them about me, shamus — that you figure I'm operating for this Morton Cotter? That I know all there is to know about Mitzi Laverick getting killed in a crash?'

'You're saying you don't?'

'What I say to you and what I'd say to the cops would be two different things, Wayne. I've warned you once. I'm warning you again. This is the last time.

Forget about the whole thing and get out of the picture.'

'Or you'll kill me?' Wayne prompted tautly.

The dark-featured man didn't answer him. He rose from his chair and adjusted his tie. He hadn't got rid of all the spilled coffee and now he wiped his coat and trousers carefully. The faint sneer came back to his mouth.

'You needn't waste any time following me, Mr. Wayne. Make good use of the time you have to make amends. Find yourself another case and another client.'

He walked out of the diner and Wayne let him reach the street. At the door he saw the stranger go to the grey Ford and unlock it before dropping onto the driving seat. The Ford was drawing away from the kerb when Wayne moved to his own car.

With the engine running he knew that something was wrong. The rear of the Plymouth had dipped at one side. He scrambled to the road and went round to look. Sure enough, one of the tyres was flat.

★ ★ ★

Maggie had news for him when he arrived back to his office in Darton City. Hank Petersen had been on again, she said. He was to ring Petersen at headquarters as soon as he got home.

Maggie began to laugh when Wayne gave her the episode of the flat tyre. She cut it short at the look on Wayne's face.

'Okay, Joey. So you don't think it's a bit funny. Neither do I when you get right down to it. But the brass nerve of the guy! Following you around the way he did. Visiting at your hotel room. Walking in on you in the diner. And if he isn't acting as a mouthpiece for one of the Cotters then who is he acting for?'

'You tell me,' Wayne grunted. 'What's eating Hank anyhow?'

He dialled police headquarters and asked for Petersen. He was put through to the sergeant in half a minute.

'Hello again, Joe. Would you mind riding down here? I've got something I'd like you to see.'

'No kidding, Hank? You wouldn't have

the case wrapped up, by any chance?'

'That's what I would call kidding,' Petersen snorted. 'Are you coming, or have you lost interest?'

'I'll be right with you, Hank.'

He arrived at Cressley Street and the City Hall buildings a short time later. The desk sergeant in the outer office jerked his thumb when he looked in.

'Hank's waiting for you, Joe.'

'With the killer?' Wayne hazarded.

'Not exactly. Go ahead and see anyhow.'

Wayne rapped at Petersen's door and was told to come in. Petersen was on a chair before his desk and Lieutenant Eckert was striding up and down the floor. Eckert halted and stared flintily at the visitor.

'What do you know about that?' he asked flatly. He was pointing at a suitcase as he spoke. The suitcase was on the desk and Wayne crossed to it.

'Go on and open it,' Petersen invited. 'I'm dying to see your face when you do.'

Wayne's grin was feeble. 'One of these trick boxes,' he chuckled. 'Open the lid and something springs out at you.'

He opened the suitcase and made a soft whistle. The suitcase was crammed with money, done up neatly with the kind of rubber bands that banks used.

14

It was a minute before Wayne could gather his scattered wits. He didn't have to be told who the owner of the money had been. He had spent the better part of two days trying to trace the stuff, and here it was, at police headquarters.

'What do you know about it, Joe?'

It was Lieutenant Eckert repeating his question. Wayne tore his eyes away from the suitcase and put them on Eckert.

'Huh?' he said. 'I don't get it. Where did you find all this dough?' His mind was functioning rapidly once more. He didn't know where the cops had found the twenty-odd thousand. He didn't know how much the cops knew of his own search for the money. He decided to play it cool and make caution his ally.

Eckert lit a cigarette and blew a stream of smoke from his nostrils. He was holding his impatience in check.

'That's not answering my question,' he

reminded Wayne. 'Do I have to dig an answer out of you?'

Hank Petersen's eyes had a cold twinkle as he watched Wayne. 'Maybe he's just suffered a bad shock, Lieutenant. Maybe we ought to give him a few minutes to get over it.'

'That's right,' Eckert said thinly. 'So he can dream up a story to extend his bluff?'

The suggestion of a grin plucked at Joe Wayne's mouth.

'You don't really mean it, Lieutenant. When did I ever pull a bluff on the department? When was I ever anything but a good and co-operative guy with the department?'

Eckert moved his shoulders and evaded his gaze.

'Okay, Joe, so you're the policeman's ideal of the private investigator.' He sighed and jerked his head at a chair. 'Sit down, Joe.'

'But I'm a very busy man, Lieutenant — '

'You're not interested in the suitcase? You're not interested in the dough? Do you know anything about it? Do you know all that's worth knowing about it?'

Wayne sobered and pushed his hat up on his head. He poked a cigarette to his lips and lit it. He glanced at the expectant Petersen.

'Have you made a count?'

'Twenty-four thousand bucks, with a little left over for petty cash.'

'Then it does figure.'

'We hoped it would figure for somebody,' Eckert urged. His voice had softened and he drew up a chair in front of Wayne. 'Do you know who owned the money?'

'I can't swear to it, but I could make a reasonably good guess. What beats me is where it came from, after — '

'After you'd scoured the town trying to find it?' Eckert said gently. 'After you shifted out to Ashbury when you failed to find it here?'

An inspiration hit Wayne. 'Then the dark-faced guy — ' He realised he had made a mistake. The dark-skinned man couldn't possibly have been a cop put to following him. 'But no. It must have been somebody else.'

'What dark-faced guy are you talking about?' Petersen asked sharply.

Eckert waved a hand at Petersen. 'Take it easy, Hank. It's plain to see he's moving around on an elevated level. Let him come back to earth gradually. Who did you figure for the owner of the dough, Joe?'

'Mitzi Laverick, of course.'

'Of course!' Petersen echoed with a grimace. 'Just like that! I told you he moves about three streets ahead of the department all the time.'

Wayne glanced at him again. 'Knock it off, Hank. I thought I had a good lead. Find the dough, I thought, and the killer is about six inches away. Where did you find the dough?'

'We found it at the first place you should have looked when you got the idea,' Eckert explained. 'The dame's apartment on Comstock Avenue. She must have planned to stash it for a while.'

It was a shock for Wayne and no mistake. His grin turned wry. 'Well, I'll be a horned toad. But that doesn't seem logical. The girl was set on pulling her freight out of town. The way she behaved when I talked with her she never wanted to see Darton City again in her life. Naturally I assumed she wouldn't be leaving anything worth while behind when she did pull out. It just goes to show you, I guess. You can't be the winner all of the time. I — ' He broke off when another thought struck him. 'The money was in her apartment, you say? Where did you find it?'

'Under a loose floorboard,' Eckert explained with a touch of smugness. Before he could continue Hank Petersen stole his thunder.

'All thanks to you we did find it, Joe,' he said. 'It was your activity that put us on to it.'

Eckert looked annoyed now. Wayne waited for Petersen to elaborate. The lieutenant beat him to it.

'What put you to sniffing for money in the first place? That's the point that puzzles me a little. Also,' he added with a hint of stiffness in his tone, 'I understood there was to be full co-operation with the police department on your part.'

'I didn't want to make smoke until I was sure,' Wayne told them. 'I got a hunch about the car. I wondered if Mitzi had bought the car herself, or if someone else had bought it and made her a present of it. I had a look at it and followed the sales sticker to the place where it was bought. The guy in charge was willing to help — after he'd contacted you, of course. And I take it you just sat back and waited for developments to take place. Am I right, Lieutenant?'

'Go on,' Eckert said woodenly. 'We're not sure if there's a medal to suit your case.'

'I don't want a medal, Lieutenant. All I want is to put the finger on Mitzi Laverick's slayer. Who is, incidentally, if the fact had escaped you, also the punk who tried to make past tense out of yours truly when he was about it.'

Petersen took up his tale.

'You heard that the dame had paid cash for the car, so you asked yourself where she might have got it from. From there you moved in on the banks in town — '

'Which of them put you wise?' Wayne asked him.

'Merchants and Western Consolidated,' Eckert contributed. 'Milner, the manager, thought there was something funny about your call. He let us know. It was the first time we knew the dame had so much money on hand. What did it smell like to you, Joe?'

'Blackmail,' Wayne admitted. 'She must have been squeezing some guy and put the pressure on once too often.'

Eckert knocked ash from his cigarette.

'It's how we see it also. When you didn't find what you wanted in Darton City, you went on to Ashbury. That was pretty smart of you too. Ashbury was where Mitzi Laverick hired you to take her safely. Did you come up with anything for your trouble?'

Wayne hesitated over that one. Petersen helped him to make up his mind.

'You spoke of a dark-faced guy. What did you mean, Joe, a foreigner of some kind?'

Wayne shook his head. He told them of the visit to his hotel of the dark-skinned man, and what had passed between them. Eckert leaned forward with fresh interest.

'That would be the guy that spoke to Lashlin after the crash at the bend. The guy you asked Lashlin about afterwards. Is that so?'

'Lashlin's a cute cookie too,' Wayne said drily.

'Lashlin does his duty. Maybe we could make something out of your friend, Joe. He tailed you to Ashbury. He watched you go around the banks.'

'I saw him again today,' Wayne said. He realised there was no point in holding anything back. Besides, the police might have a clue to the identity of the stranger. When he had finished Hank Petersen slammed his fist on the desk.

'We want that guy, Lieutenant.' He wheeled to the door of the office. 'I'll get out a flyer at once — '

'Hold on,' Eckert snapped at him. 'Slow down, Hank. At the minute it's Joe here he's showing interest in. If we set up a search it might put him to ground and we'll never find him.'

'So what do we do?' Petersen complained. 'I've talked with Mort Cotter. I've talked with Frank Cotter. Frank says he never heard of the two guys that waited for Joe at Sally Rogan's apartment.'

'He said that?' Wayne murmured. 'Did he also say that he never heard of Mitzi Laverick?'

Petersen nodded. 'He nearly laughed his head off. He didn't know the dame. He might have seen her at one of the clubs he and Mort run. If he did he didn't give her a second glance.'

'He's a liar on one count at least, Hank. I followed those goons to his house on Huxley Park. If he'll tell lies about that he'll tell lies about anything.'

'I know. These Cotter guys have been riding close to the edge for a long time. But suspicion is one thing, Joe, and proof is another. So where do you go from here?'

Wayne glanced from one man to another. The expression on Eckert's face was lugubrious.

'What is this turning into anyhow, boys

— some kind of band of hope? I'm a loner, remember. I don't run with a pack. It has advantages in that you don't have to take orders from anyone but yourself.'

'You're doing nicely,' Eckert complimented. 'What's the matter with continuing to string along?'

'String along, he says! The nerve of some cops. Look, Lieutenant, what you're really searching for just now is a decoy. And who better to fill the bill than little old Joe Wayne? What has Wayne got to lose but his neck — '

'Or his licence,' Eckert amended cryptically.

Wayne slid to his feet, cheeks starting to burn.

'Who's going to deprive me of my licence? What grounds do you have for depriving me of my licence? I've got a good mind to see — '

'He's only kidding, Joe,' Hank Petersen said weakly. He was surprised at Eckert's remark.

'I'm not kidding,' Eckert retorted firmly. 'I'm trying to tell him that he's in this gag to his eyeballs. I'm trying to impress on him that he can't walk out and forget the whole thing. Even if he wants to.'

'But you don't want to,' Petersen appealed to Wayne. 'You just said — '

'I know what I just said, Hank.' Wayne's eyes locked with those of Eckert. There was a glimmer of mockery in the lieutenant now. 'You are looking for a decoy, aren't you?'

'To be quite frank, Joe — '

'Don't bother being frank,' Wayne said curtly. 'I understand a little of your psychology, Lieutenant. Okay, I'm in for better or worse. What do you want me to do?'

'You'll do it?' Eckert asked hopefully.

'I'll think about it. What's the joke?'

'I've got it weighed up,' the lieutenant went on with new enthusiasm. 'I'm saying this killer is one of the Cotters, or is closely connected with the Cotters. So far we've gone as close to tramping on their toes as we dare without real evidence against them. If we pursue the matter any further — officially that is — it could earn the whole department a smart rap over the knuckles from the D.A.'s office, or even from Mort's lawyer. But with a free agent on the ball — '

'I'm beginning to wise up,' Wayne broke in on him. 'Any dirt that would be thrown would naturally attach itself to me. But what about my reputation? And what if I run foul of the Cotters' lawyers? Where does it put me, besides out on a long limb with anybody that means anything in this town?'

Some of the light faded from Eckert's eye. He turned to Hank Petersen and shrugged.

'It's too much to ask of him, Hank.'

'Not if I know Joe, it's not,' Petersen grinned. 'Be reasonable, Joe. All it involves is going ahead with your case. The only variation is that you'll be working closely with me. Immediately you caught a whisper of value you'd pass it along. And if I'd happen to give orders — ' He stopped speaking at the frown on Wayne's face. 'All right, don't call it orders. Call it giving you some advice. Why not, Joe? You were involved with the dead dame. You've got a certain responsibility to her brother who hired you. And as you've just said, you want to catch this killer as badly as we do. So what do you say?'

Wayne mulled it over for a minute. He could see the fix the police were in. Although the Cotter brothers were probably little better than sewer rats they still rated in the eyes of their own social circle, and still commanded a degree of respect and immunity from the upper strata of the city's administration.

'Okay. I might be the biggest dope out of a straitjacket, but I'll give it a whirl. On one condition though. I make my own rules. I have all the room I need to spread myself. I don't have any of your soft-shoes inhibiting me. Does that meet with your approval?'

'You sure you wouldn't like my badge?' Eckert said with a touch of sourness.

'I wouldn't touch your badge on a gold plate, Lieutenant. I don't trust you any more than about half the length I could throw you with lead weights on your feet. But having the blessing of your department might be a nice change in the weather. Take it or leave it.'

'I'll take it,' Eckert said grudgingly. 'It's not exactly what I had in mind, but I suppose we have to make some allowances for your eccentricity.'

'Initiative, Lieutenant. Pure and simple. Now, could I dig up a slice of information on the Cotters? I did visit with Morton, as Hank knows. Hank knows too the sort of reception I got from Mort. I didn't have time to find out if it was Friday or Christmas day before I hit the front door-step on my ego. Brother Frank I can't even recall eating off the same plate with. I wouldn't know him if I met him on the street.'

Eckert lit another cigarette and passed a hand over his head. Just then he looked mildly apprehensive. It was plain he was wondering if he had been too impulsive in asking the investigator to help him.

'What do you want to know?' Eckert said.

'Take Mort first. Is he married?'

'He is. Nice woman too. Quiet, modest. Not like Mort at all. She'd take it bad if she found out Mort was playing around with one of his canaries.'

'There's no proof that he was. How about Frank? Has he got himself a homely and modest wife too?'

'Frank isn't married,' Eckert told him. 'Both of them have a crowd of toughs as hangers-on. Frank denied that any of his boys went after you. They're in a racket where they have to surround themselves with hardcases.'

'All right,' Wayne said and started for the door. 'I feel an inch lower than a snail's belly taking direction from you fellows. But if it lets us wind up with the slayer of Mitzi Laverick, even that taste will wash out of my mouth in time.'

'One thing more,' Eckert said soberly. 'We haven't given you a licence to act rough. We'll not be sitting on our tails while you're doing all the work either. Just in case the sense of power goes to your head. You understand?'

Wayne's mouth curled. 'I think so. I think too I'm being taken for a sucker.' He nodded in the direction of the suitcase. 'What will you do with it?'

'Keep it here until we find the guy who

shelled out. I want to see his face when we spring it on him.'

'If you find him,' Wayne said and left the room.

Maggie Yarmon had gone home when he reached the office. But Maggie had left a note to give her a ring if he needed anything extra attended to.

Wayne sat in his office for a half hour and smoked. He had the feeling that the dark-skinned man wasn't far away, that it wouldn't be long until he heard from him again. Was the man a bluffer or in earnest? he wondered. It was a stupid thing to ask himself, he knew, and he would be crazy if he didn't treat the stranger and his threats in all seriousness.

He was considering grabbing a meal before going home to a cool drink and a shower when the phone on Maggie's desk rang. The caller was Ruth Foran and she asked Wayne if he was doing anything special that evening.

'I don't know, honey,' he answered slowly. 'I've got myself stuck on this case and I can't get off it.'

'You're talking about the Mitzi Laverick affair, I suppose? Has nobody been caught yet for the murder?'

'Not up to the moment, Ruth. The whole thing has turned out to be a bit of a puzzle.'

'I see.' Ruth sounded disappointed. 'So we can't have dinner together after all. I did have something nice planned for you, Joe. Would you care to hear about it?'

'Over the phone? Baby, do me a favour.'

Ruth laughed and Wayne smiled while he listened to it. He depended on the girl more than he cared to admit. It was good to know that one thing at least was solid and reliable in the hectic and confused world he moved around in.

'When do I see you then, Joe — tomorrow, next week, next year, never?'

'Tomorrow evening, honey. Come snowstorm or earthquake, we'll make it a date. But, honey . . . '

'Yes?'

'If something really important crops up I'll give you a tinkle.'

'All right, Joe, I get the message. I'll expect you when I see you. Goodbye.'

'Wait, honey, I didn't — '

A click told him that Ruth had hung up.

He had a meal and went home to Vine. He relaxed with the TV until dark. Then he went down to the Plymouth and drove off through the neon-lit streets. Once again his destination was Morton Cotter's house on Columbus Avenue.

15

Columbus Avenue after dark was scarcely recognisable as the same place he had visited in daylight. The street lamps were spaced at wide intervals and threw off a meagre glow that gave an eerie, muted effect which could have been borrowed from a nineteenth-century stage melo-drama. Perhaps it was an atmosphere that suited the mood of the local residents, Wayne thought. The local residents were well heeled and could afford all sorts of overtones, dramatic or any other kind.

He found the drive leading to *Green-mere* but took the Plymouth past it for a couple of hundred yards. When he had switched off the engine and killed the headlights he sat for a time and looked around him. As far as he could see, his was the only car parked on the street. The radio had been playing gently and now he twisted the knob and listened with the window wound down.

Five minutes went by and no other traffic came into the avenue behind him. He lit a cigarette and thought of his interview with Petersen and Eckert. Of course they were using him as a decoy. They might know more about the case to date than they had told him. They might even have the killer of Mitzi Laverick marked and under constant surveillance. They were pretending to hold their hand while Wayne moved around in the open, in the hope, likely, that the killer of the girl might pick the investigator as his next victim.

Since when had the cops to depend on the manoeuvres of a private detective? Wayne thought sourly. And while he was in a reflective frame of mind, just what had caused him to return to Morton Cotter's house in the cover of darkness?

Curiosity was as good an answer as any, he tried to convince himself. It was the curious operator who obtained results. It was the curious operator who kept the quarry on the move until he shifted to the open. It could be the curious operator too, he decided grimly, who would finish up in the teeth of that Alsatian if he wasn't careful.

With this last eventuality in mind Wayne fondled the .38 in its shoulder holster. He let another few minutes ride by. He was about to get out of the car when headlights forked into the avenue from the opposite end. The vehicle was moving rapidly however, and went on past without reducing its speed. Wayne didn't step out until it had left the avenue by the end he had used to come in.

He locked the car and strolled to the entrance of the driveway to *Greenmere*. Beyond the entrance she shadows were really dense. A single lamp burned at the front of the house; there were no lamps burning in the rooms at this side.

When he drew level with the front of the house he halted. He was at this point on his last trip when the Alsatian had bounded towards him. The night was quiet; the house was quiet. Just what did he hope to salvage from this dangerous caper?

He had half a mind to go on to the front door now and ask to see Morton

Cotter again. There was a lot that he could discuss with the night-club owner if Cotter was willing to be reasonable. Cotter could be out, of course. It was very probable that he was out somewhere, supervising the workings of the fun houses he ran.

While Wayne hesitated he fancied he heard a sound sifting from the rear of the building. He twisted his head the better to listen. There it was again, the low, distressed sobbing of a woman.

He couldn't have held back now if he'd wanted to. Instinctively his legs took him slowly to the side of the house and on to the far corner. Here was a huge sun-porch with strong lights blazing. The sun-porch gave onto a vast stretch of lawn where the musical tinkle of a fountain came off the flower-scented air.

There was nobody in the sun-porch that Wayne could see. Frowning, he squinted across the shadowy lawn. When his eyes became accustomed to the mixture of light and gloom he made out the shape of a woman. She was sitting on a bench close to an archway that was covered in climbing roses.

Something right out of Zola.

Even as Wayne studied the sun-porch again the woman's sobbing lifted once more.

There was no one on the lawn with her that he could see, so it couldn't be said that anyone was beating her around or calling her names. But who was the woman — Cotter's wife?

Boldly, Wayne cut away from the pathway and entered a cluster of shrubbery. He worked his way carefully to a point that gave him a view of the bench and the woman's back. Now she was using a handkerchief on her eyes. Now she was taking a cigarette from a case and lighting it.

She was quiet as she puffed. From this angle Wayne now had a clear view of the sun-porch. It was empty, as he had thought it was, but a door leading on to the rear of the house stood open. Through there were more lights. There was no one to be seen however.

Suddenly a low baying came from a scattering of buildings on Wayne's left. He noticed that the woman froze at the sound and twisted her head quickly. The baying became a chorus of soft barking. Wayne felt cold sweat lifting to his brow. The dog or dogs didn't seem to be coming any closer and he tried to relax.

He was attempting to get nearer to the woman on the bench when she bounded to her feet and faced into his direction.

'Who's there?'

The voice was taut and high-pitched; there was no trace of fear in it. Wayne caught his lip in his teeth and waited, hoping the woman would think she was mistaken.

'Who's there, I say? Is it you, Rafe? Why are you skulking around like this?'

Wayne shifted slowly to the open.

'It's not whom you think it is, Mrs. Cotter. It is Mrs. Cotter, I believe?'

The woman appeared to freeze for a single instant, then she half turned as if to flee. Wayne spoke rapidly.

'Please don't be alarmed. I intended calling on your husband. I was walking to the front when I thought I heard someone crying. I could have been mistaken, but — '

'Who are you?'

Wayne was close enough to have a look at her now. She was tall and had a good shape. She was clad in a short dress and had a wrap about her shoulders. Her hair reached the shoulders and was curled up at the ends. The eyes that stared at Wayne were dark and sparkling. When he didn't answer immediately she stamped her foot.

'Are you going to say who you are and how you come to be skulking about here?'

'I've just told you.'

'I don't believe you. Look, mister, I'm going to scream. I'm going to scream and keep on screaming until Rafe turns the dogs loose.'

'I don't mind if they're poodles, Mrs. Cotter, but not the Alsatian, please . . . '

'Then you've been here before? I know! You're a policeman. But why couldn't you announce yourself in the proper fashion?'

'I'm not a policeman. I'm a private investigator. My name is Joseph Wayne. As I said, I heard you crying. I wouldn't be worth my salt if I didn't investigate a crying lady, would I now, Mrs. Cotter?'

'But I wasn't — ' she started to say and broke off. She blinked a moment and patted at her eyes with her handkerchief. Then she puffed from her cigarette. 'If Morton finds you here he'll be very angry, Mr. Wayne,' she said instead.

'The police have been hounding him — '

'Do you know why?'

'Of course I know why. Because of that girl who was murdered. Oh, they tried to keep it off me, but I'm not stupid. The girl worked at one of Morton's clubs, didn't she?'

'You never met her, Mrs. Cotter?'

'I never met her. Why should I have met her — Yes! I see what you mean. The general opinion is that Morton was having an affair with the girl, that she wouldn't be bought off the easy way. So he — But it isn't true, Mr. Wayne! I know. I'm telling you! Morton wouldn't stoop to such a thing.'

She shivered as though she was feeling the evening chill. She drew the wrap closer about her shoulders. Wayne brought a cigarette out and lit it.

'Why were you crying, Mrs. Cotter?'

'It's none of your — All right! I — I had a row with Morton, if you must know. I lost my head, I guess. I can't bear the strain for much longer.'

'I'm sorry. But if you're so sure that your husband didn't have anything to do with the girl, why did you fight with him because of her?'

'What the hell is going on there?' a harsh voice ripped from the direction of the sun-porch.

'You'd better go!' the woman hissed. 'He said he would turn the dogs on the next person who came asking questions . . .'

'Julia! Who is that man with you?' Cotter demanded. He began walking quickly towards them. The woman moaned.

'Run!'

'Take it easy,' Wayne urged. 'The dogs aren't loose yet.'

He stood still while Morton Cotter halted before him. There was a gun in the hand of the night-club owner and the muzzle was directed at Wayne's chest. A throttled curse emerged from him when he recognised the intruder.

'By heaven, it's you again!'

'So you know him,' Julia Cotter said tonelessly. 'There's no need to get rough with him, Morton. He doesn't mean any harm. I wish you had gone when I told you to leave, Mr. Wayne.'

'Leave us alone,' Cotter grated at his wife. 'Was he asking you questions? Did you tell him anything?'

'He wasn't asking questions. What could I tell him? Why don't you give them the truth and be done with it? If it is the truth, what have you to worry about?'

For an instant Wayne thought Cotter would strike the woman. He prepared to lunge at him, gun or no gun, if he did. Cotter appeared to gain control of himself.

'How did you get in here?' he growled at Wayne.

'I walked in.'

'You sneaked in would be more like it,' was the acid response. 'Didn't you ever hear of a front door?'

'Yeah, I have. I was heading for it when I thought I heard someone crying. It must have been your wife crying,' he added slowly while he watched the man.

The gun jerked closer to him. Cotter was breathing shallowly. 'You nosey creep,' he rasped. 'Go into the house, Julia.'

'But Morton — '

'I said to go into the house. We'll talk later. Did you catch him sneaking around?'

'No, no! He just walked over the lawn and asked if anything was wrong. You won't do anything rash, Morton . . . '

'Do I ever do anything rash?' he rejoined impatiently. 'Please go into the house.'

'Very well.'

The woman was reluctant to move. Her gaze lingered for another instant on Wayne, then she wheeled abruptly and walked to the sun-porch. She walked gracefully and with her head in the air.

'Thoroughbred all through.'

'What in blazes are you talking about?'

'Your wife, Mr. Cotter. She's a nice

woman. A woman like that shouldn't have to sit all alone on the lawn at night and weep.'

Cotter's laugh was a harsh bellow of derision.

'You classify yourself as an all-round expert. How would you like to be a dead all-round expert?'

'I'd find it very tedious. Being dead, I mean. There's so much of interest going on, it would be a pity to be cut out of the picture.'

'I'm glad you have that much sense. What brought you here in the first place?'

'I'm not sure. I wanted to talk with you, I guess.'

'About what?'

'I think you know well enough, Mr. Cotter. I'm a working man. The people who hire me give me no rest. I'm supposed to keep going all day and all night. The most I can hope for in the line of reward is a bite from a dog or a bite from some angry guy like you.'

'You think you're slick, don't you? You think you're making me sweat by crawling back here again when I warned you off. I

don't know who killed Mitzi Laverick.
I've told the police so. I told them to leave
me alone or I'll trample all over their
necks. Now I'm telling you to leave me
alone or I'll put a bullet in you and say I
thought you were a burglar.'

'I get the gist. And they tell me that a
guy who kills once can kill twice without
dropping more than about six tears over
it.'

'Curse you, Wayne. I haven't killed
anybody.'

Wayne took a drag on his cigarette.
Cotter's gun was aimed at his face now. It
was a time for extreme caution, but
Wayne had a belief that once you lit a fire
under a suspect it ought to be kept stoked
until he began to steam.

'So you say, Mr. Cotter. I'd like to
believe you. I'd like to pass you by and be
able to forget about you. I can't get you
out of my mind. You must have heard that
a couple of goofs waited for me at Sally
Rogan's apartment and tried to discour-
age me from getting acquainted with
Sally. They shouldn't have bothered,
because Sally can't tell anything about

Mitzi Laverick that I can't tell myself.'

'I know nothing about any men who waited for you. Are you going to leave?'

'You don't give me any choice.'

'That's got an ominous ring to it, Wayne. I'm telling you for the last time — '

'You just think it's the last time, Mr. Cotter. And as for the jerk you've put to following me, you'd better teach him the rudiments of his job. Next time he crosses my path I'm going to make him a very sorry guy.'

Wayne had turned off across the lawn when Cotter spoke sharply after him.

'Wait! Who are you talking about? I haven't put anybody to following you. If I wanted you out of my hair you'd never know what hit you.'

Wayne halted to face him again. The gun wasn't held quite so high now.

'I guess it's your brother I ought to see then. Thanks for the tip, Mr. Cotter.'

'Hold on, damn you,' Cotter snarled when he started walking again.

Wayne strove to keep his excitement at bay.

'For what? You'd like me to be facing you when you shoot me. Is that it? Then you can say I was coming at you when you had to defend yourself.'

It seemed he had gone too far. The gun in Cotter's hand swept up again. His face was a dull, angry blob in the shadows.

'I'll say one thing for you, you've got nerve.'

'Maybe I'm tired of cringing for the second kick. Maybe I don't give a spit for you or your gun. If you call it nerve I can't stop you.'

Cotter made a gesture with his head.

'Come into the house.'

'Ahuh! So it's to be the dungeons after all. Thanks, Mr. Cotter, but I think I've got an attack of claustrophobia coming on. I'm really an outdoors boy at heart.'

'You wish to talk about Mitzi Laverick?' Cotter demanded huskily. 'Do you or don't you?'

'You know what I want to talk about. But if you'd give me a choice right now — '

'Come into the house,' Cotter repeated. He made a motion towards the sun-porch with the gun.

Wayne's hesitation was momentary. He walked slowly towards the light. He went through a large door and saw Julia Cotter standing in a hallway. The woman was smoking another cigarette. She looked quite composed and in command of herself.

'What do you intend to do?' she said to Cotter.

'What the hell can I do?' he retorted. 'And don't get hysterical on me again. You understand?'

She nodded and Wayne walked past her. When he turned his head Cotter had put his gun away.

'Into the library. Third door on your left.'

The door was open and Wayne entered the large room. Cotter followed him and closed the door behind him.

'Sit down. There's a drink on the table if you want it.'

'Thanks. I could use one.'

He poured himself a drink, whisky over

ice. He swirled it around for a moment before drinking it. He took one of the easy chairs and started a cigarette. He stared at Cotter who had lifted the telephone receiver and was dialling. His face was pale and taut, the eyes cold and intent.

'Who are you calling — the cops?'

Cotter didn't answer him.

'Hello,' he said into the receiver. 'This is Mort. Put Frank on, will you?' A half minute later, 'Look, Frank, this private eye is here again. Yeah, I know! It's no good, I tell you. I've a hunch he's in cahoots with the cops. I've had a bagful of it, Frank. You're taking it from here on in. It's the only way . . . I've got a reputation. Maybe it stinks a little, but it's still a reputation. No! You'll do it. The whole works. I mean it, Frank. When? Right away!'

Cotter hung up. He moved to a button on the wall and pressed it. The door opened and the two men in tan slacks and tweed jackets entered. They stared at Wayne and the .38 he was holding on the three of them.

'See he gets to Frank,' Cotter told them. 'Don't worry. He won't shoot. He'd be signing his own death warrant if he did.'

16

The one called Nate got into the Plymouth with Wayne; Rod rode behind in another car. Nate let smoke dribble from his lips as he watched Wayne.

'Don't try any tricks,' he said. 'I didn't like you in the beginning and I don't like you now.'

'Let's drop the sex-appeal angle,' Wayne told him. 'Nobody wants you to like me, and when I want to be admired I prefer it to be done by dames.'

'You think you're cute.'

'I think I'm a riot. I think you're a riot. I think the whole shebang at *Greenmere* could take lessons on how to become civilised.'

At the end of Columbus Avenue Wayne gave the steering wheel a left-hand twist.

'Where do you figure you're going? Huxley Park is in the opposite direction.'

'Why didn't you say so?' Wayne flipped the wheel round.

'You're just acting the clown, Wayne. You know the way. Don't make any deviations.'

They drove for five minutes in silence. Wayne glanced in the mirror and saw the other car close to his tail. He had begun to sweat again. He should have kept his gun on them back there. He should have held them covered until he called in for Petersen or Eckert. Why did they want him to visit Mort Cotter's brother? Was Frank the guilty one, and Mort wished Frank to wrap up his own dirty work?

'Did you know Mitzi Laverick?' he said presently to Nate.

'What does it matter. I didn't kill her.'

'But you know who did — huh?'

'Keep quiet and keep driving,' he was ordered. 'If I had my way I'd put a rock to your neck and drop you in the ocean.'

'So you don't go for private eyes. What sort of people do you go for, chum?'

Nate didn't answer him. He was concentrating on the road ahead in case Wayne deliberately took a wrong turning. Traffic in mid-town was thick and Wayne had the notion to crash his car into another one. That would get him company for sure, and bring on the cops with a vengeance.

'Go carefully,' Nate warned as though he could read his mind. 'You're to be delivered at *Montcalm* and you're going to be delivered.'

It seemed all too short a time since they'd started off from *Greenmere* till they were cruising onto the smooth surface of Huxley Park. Wayne slowed on the approach to the *Montcalm* driveway. In the mirror he saw Rod sliding his car up behind him.

'Do we stop here or go up to the house?'

'Straight to the house. Stop at the front door.'

'Does Frank keep any Alsatians, do you know?'

'He keeps apes,' Nate chuckled drily. 'If you don't mind your manners he might turn you over to them.'

Wayne took the Plymouth onto the driveway. There were three cars parked opposite a flight of steps. Lights burned in two rooms on the ground floor, but the shades were drawn. Wayne killed the engine and waited. Rod drove up alongside the Plymouth and scrambled out. Wayne was opening his door when Nate told him to stay where he was.

'But I figured we were going visiting.'

'Take it easy.'

Rod mounted the steps and pressed on a bell-push. Wayne watched while the door opened and a man in a dark suit and white shirt appeared. Rod spoke with him before passing inside. The door closed and Nate drummed on his knee with his fingers.

'What do we do now?' Wayne queried. 'This mightn't be Frank's night for investigators. Look, Nate, couldn't we drop the whole thing and take off for home?'

Wayne was reaching for his gun when Nate beat him to it. He spoke thickly through his teeth.

'We're acting decent with you, shamus. Don't strain the good relations effort too far.'

At that minute the door opened again and Rod came out. He descended the steps quickly to the Plymouth. Before Wayne could say anything he made a gesture.

'Okay, let's go.'

'Home?'

'Later maybe. It depends on Frank.' Rod was sneering as he said that. Nate prodded Wayne's ribs with his gun.

'Go on, pal. You're on your own from here.' He slipped out of the Plymouth behind Wayne and went over to the other car.

Wayne climbed the steps and was greeted by an elderly butler. At some time or other the butler's nose had been in an argument with a hefty fist. He held the door wide and inclined his head slightly. There was a glint in his eye that Wayne didn't care for.

'Mr. Cotter is waiting to see you,' he announced.

He took Wayne through a hallway, through a lounge that was the last word in luxury and bad taste. Here was an oak door which the butler rapped and opened.

'Mr. Wayne, sir . . . '

'Come in, Wayne.'

The room Wayne entered was furnished to serve the function of office or study. There was a rug on the centre of the floor, a large desk on one side of the room that had shelves of books behind it. Four easy chairs were scattered around. On one of them a rugged looking character in slacks and sweater sat reading a magazine. On the chair nearest the door a tall, fair-headed man was sitting with a cigar in his mouth.

He stood up as Wayne entered and brought the cigar from his lips. He had Morton Cotter's light blue eyes, and, like Morton's, they tended to bulge. He was much younger than his brother, much more handsome. He regarded the visitor shrewdly and extended a manicured hand.

'Hello, Wayne. I'm glad you came.'

'I didn't think I had much of a choice.'

Wayne held the hand briefly and let it go. His gaze shifted to the other man reading the magazine. Whatever he was reading, he seemed to find it more interesting than the newcomer. He had gum in his mouth and chewed it as he flicked over a page.

'That's Benny,' Cotter said with a faint grin. 'You don't have to worry about him.'

'That so? Is it okay if I worry about him anyhow, just the same?'

Benny raised his head and gave Wayne a cold stare.

'Have you solved any good cases lately?'

'Say, that's good. Can he do any more tricks?'

'Forget it,' Cotter said with a hint of annoyance. 'You might not believe it, but I've got a few enemies. I keep Benny around so I can sleep good at nights.'

'I see. And how are you sleeping these nights, Mr. Cotter? Or could I call you Frank?'

Cotter let his breath slide out of his teeth. He waved towards a chair. 'Sit down. This might take a few minutes to get straight. I'm not in the habit of talking with private detectives, and I'm not sure how to begin. You must understand,' he went on slowly when Wayne was seated, 'I'm not afraid of you in any way.'

'I wish I could say I'm not afraid of you, Frank. I'm quaking in my shoes. It's no wonder Benny there can't concentrate on the cheesecake pictures. But if you're planning on killing me,' Wayne continued, 'I must warn you that I've got friends at police headquarters. They mightn't like you killing me. Somebody nearly did it on the Ashbury road.'

Wayne noticed that Frank Cotter caught his breath and that a nerve in his cheek twitched. He closed his eyes for an instant as if to wipe out a distasteful memory. Wayne thought it odd that he hadn't been frisked before coming in here. So far both Morton and Frank had handled him with a carelessness hardly in keeping with a bunch of killers. It could all be part of an elaborate bluff, of course, designed to throw him off guard until they had assessed his potential properly.

'You're working on the murder of the girl?' Cotter said.

'That's right. So are the cops. They allowed me to take an interest on account of my involvement with Mitzi Laverick.'

'Have you made any progress so far?'

Wayne stared at him before answering.

'It's difficult to say. I've been trying to establish a definite lead. At the minute I'm just asking around.'

'You suspect Morton or me of knowing something about the murder, don't you, Wayne?'

The man with the magazine squinted over the edge of it and waited for an answer. Frank Cotter leaned forward on his chair and puffed gently at his cigar.

'Do you?' Wayne said.

Cotter shrugged. The faint smile that twisted his lips was tinged with bitterness.

'Why should I answer you? If I say no, you'll merely assume that I'm lying. You suspected Morton first of all, didn't you? Maybe you still suspect him. Maybe you think we're giving you some kind of runaround.'

Wayne said drily, 'The thought never entered my head. But if you are you're only wasting your time. Could I ask you something else, Frank?'

Cotter nodded. Benny rustled his magazine in agitation.

'Why am I a big thing in your life all of

a sudden, Frank? First visit I made to your brother he couldn't get me out of the joint fast enough. He treated me like a speck of dust had settled on his toecap.

'When I called again tonight I had a gun pushed in my puss, sure. But Morton lacked his old sting. I found his wife crying in the back garden. She was worried about Mitzi Laverick too. Morton asked me in and got on the phone to you, then he told his pet monkeys to bring me here. Why?'

'I thought I ought to talk with you, Wayne. As I said, I'm not scared of you — '

'But you could be scared of the cops? You might even think that the cops are watching you day and night. I think they might be too. I'm not saying you're scared of me, Frank. In your book I'm a mote in your eye that you need to get rid of without lowering your status. How am I doing this far?'

Cotter puffed steadily at his cigar for a moment. Benny had given up trying to concentrate and was watching Wayne with ill-concealed distaste.

'I don't know why you're bothering,' he said to Frank Cotter. 'If I were you I wouldn't tell him a thing.'

'You're not me. I'm not asking for your opinion. Look, Benny, leave us alone for a few minutes.'

'But he might — '

'He won't.'

Benny rose from his chair and threw his magazine down. He had second thoughts about it and lifted it again. He gave Wayne a bleak stare on his way to the door. Cotter didn't speak until the door closed behind him.

'I'm going to tell you a story,' he said hesitantly. 'Not because I'm afraid of you or the police — '

'If it's a good story why haven't you given it to the police already?'

Cotter regarded him for ten seconds. He answered curtly. 'It was you that Mitzi turned to in the first place. You were in the car with her when it crashed.'

Wayne drew a sharp breath. 'Then you did know her? But your brother said — '

'Never mind what he said. Because she worked at the Jackpot you naturally linked her up with Mort. You linked her up with the wrong guy, Wayne. It happens that I knew Mitzi . . . Pretty well too.'

'I see,' Wayne murmured. The whole affair smelled suspiciously of an act to lead him astray, to add to his confusion. 'How well did you know her?'

'I was in love with her.'

Had he hit Wayne in the stomach he couldn't have shaken him more. Cotter was quick to read his revulsion and his disbelief. His lips twisted again.

'You find that hard to accept?'

'I'm trying to cope with it. You were in love with Mitzi Laverick? Then — then you must have known that — '

'She was going to have a baby?' Cotter finished for him. There was a pained and haunted look in his eyes now. If he was putting on an act he was putting all he had into it. Still, Wayne was sceptical of his sincerity. He had mixed with enough of Cotter's stripe to know they would pull out all the stops in their efforts to wriggle off the hook. But if what Frank Cotter had told him was true . . .

'This is really washing day, isn't it,

Frank?' he said. 'But you're not going to confess too that you would have been the father of her baby?'

Cotter walked over to the table and stubbed out his cigar on a tray. He selected a fresh one from a box. Before lighting it he lifted the box invitingly.

'Thanks, no. I've got to watch what I cultivate.'

Cotter closed the lid of the box and sat on the edge of the table. His gaze was steady when it touched Wayne's again.

'Yes,' he said calmly, 'the baby would have been mine.'

'And you loved her?'

'I loved her.'

'Then why couldn't you marry her? You aren't married already? I'm told that you're not, so if you were in love with the girl what was to prevent you from marrying her? Why was it necessary to try and buy her off?'

Cotter's laugh was explosive and scornful.

'Buy her off! It shows what you really know, mister. You think you're a pretty smart guy. The cops think they're pretty smart guys. Well, here's something you never heard of.'

He told his story simply and in a monotone that escaped Wayne. Every word that came out of his mouth was picked up by Wayne, examined, evaluated. Wayne never took his eyes off him while he talked.

Frank Cotter had seen Mitzi Laverick for the first time five months ago in Las Vegas. Mitzi had been doing a singing act at a club. Cotter fell for the girl as soon as he laid eyes on her. He arranged to be introduced to her. They hit it off from the start. Frank told her of the clubs that he and his brother owned in Darton City; he asked the girl to come to Darton City with him. She refused. She was making out all right, she said. If he wanted to continue their friendship he would have to do it her way. Frank did. He was a regular visitor at the club where Mitzi worked, a regular caller at her apartment.

He asked her to marry him, but she said no. She would think about it, she promised. Finally he persuaded her to come to Darton City and take a job at the

Jackpot. It wasn't what he really wanted: he wanted her to give up singing and marry her. She kept putting him off by saying she would think about it.

'Then she sprang the big surprise on me,' he said dully. 'She said she was already married. She had run away from New York with some guy and married him. They had a row and she walked out on him. He had traced her to Darton City, found out that she was friendly with me — '

'Is this the real story or the one she gave you?' Wayne broke in.

'It was her angle,' Cotter said with bitterness. 'She said her husband would give her a divorce so she could marry me if I paid him some money.'

Wayne's eyes glinted. 'How much?'

'Ten thousand. I gave her the dough in cash. I asked her to take me to her husband so we could talk it over and reach a settlement. She refused. Then she said her husband wanted more money. Altogether I gave her around twenty-two thousand. I tried to have the husband traced. I had my boys comb the town.

They couldn't find him. I put it to Mitzi that she wasn't married at all and was taking me for a sucker. It was when she told me about the baby. She cried and got on a little. She said it would break her heart if I didn't trust her.'

'So you did trust her and believe her?'

Cotter shook his head.

'No . . . I had this feeling. I was sure that Mitzi would never marry me, even for the sake of the baby. She really wasn't the marrying type. Then some guys told me a few home truths about her. She had plenty of boy-friends. She liked plenty of boy-friends. The night before she was killed she rang me up. She said it was all off and that she was leaving town. She didn't want me to follow her. She said she was sorry about the money, but she had given it to her husband. Her husband had vanished from the address he was supposed to be at. She hoped to be able to pay back the dough some time. I told her to forget about the dough. I asked her to reconsider everything. I said I loved her.'

'But even that didn't melt her heart of stone?'

Cotter came off the desk and stubbed out the fresh cigar. 'She laughed at me,' he said flatly. 'Then she hung up.'

Wayne lit a cigarette and thought it over for a moment. What Cotter had just told him provided the most important part of the puzzle. A few pieces were still missing, but not many. He was tempted to tell Cotter about the money that had been found at Mitzi Laverick's apartment. It was really Cotter's money. He decided not to. Hank Petersen could make up his mind about the money when he heard the facts. Wayne had no doubt that Frank Cotter had given him the truth as he knew it.

'You've no idea who wanted her dead, Frank? You don't know what she was really running from when she was killed?'

Cotter shook his head again.

'All I can tell you is it wasn't me. I was cut up when I heard about it. Mort wanted me to go to the cops right away and give them the story. Mort is sure Mitzi played me for a sucker, and kept the money for herself.'

'What do you think, Frank?'

He was slow to answer. 'I don't know. It's possible. Even if she had taken me for a sucker I couldn't have hated her enough to kill her. When I knew she was through with me I tried to forget her. Do you have to tell the cops this, Wayne?'

'I guess so. But if you're telling the truth there's nothing to be worried about.' Another thought struck Wayne. 'You haven't attempted to find the killer yourself?'

'Of course not. I'd like to see him found. I hope he is found. Beyond that I don't feel anything now.'

'What about the muscle boys who waited for me to arrive at Sally Rogan's apartment, Frank? You denied any knowledge of them to the police. I followed them here to your house when they left the apartment.'

'I'm sorry if they were rough with you,' Cotter said. 'But I heard you gave as good as you got, if not better. They had orders to make the act look convincing.'

'How did you know I would be calling

at Sally's place? Why did you want to scare me off?'

'Chris Corby rang Mort from the club to tell him about your interest in Mitzi via Sally Rogan. Mort called me to see what I wanted done about it. I didn't want it to come out that I was so close to Mitzi. I guessed what you'd make of it. I guessed what the cops would make of it. I thought if you were scared plenty you might drop the case, so I sent Charley and Hector to meet you at Sally Rogan's apartment. Corby delayed Sally.'

'But Sally didn't know you were friendly with Mitzi, Frank. She didn't mention it to me at any rate. She did tell me about a guy called Ypson, though — '

'It seems Ypson was only one of a large circle of admirers. Mitzi mustn't have told Sally Rogan anything about me. I suppose she was keeping me under cover on account of the money she was taking me for.'

'When I woke up in the murder car I had a slight concussion,' Wayne said. 'I couldn't even remember who Mitzi was, so I searched her purse. She was carrying about five hundred dollars — '

'She didn't have all the money with her?' Cotter broke in. 'Then maybe she did have a husband and gave him the dough . . . '

'You mean she never told you who her husband was — his name, or anything of the sort?'

'She just said her married name was Abbott. Her husband's name was Jeremy. I searched for him plenty, but I never found him.'

'She told you nothing more? She didn't show you any photographs, a ring, a marriage licence?'

Cotter's grin was wry. His shrug was negative.

'That really puts me in the sucker class, doesn't it? A smart wheeler like Frank Cotter being taken for a ride by a two-timing dame! I did love her though,' he went on softly. 'The only dame I really fell for . . . '

'I was going to tell you what else she had in her purse when I searched it, Frank. There was a calling card. It had your brother's name and address.'

'I gave it to Mitzi in Vegas when I first met her. I didn't have a card of my own along. I remember I needed some printed and put a couple of Mort's into my wallet in case I picked up some talent.'

Wayne didn't stay much longer. Frank Cotter saw him to the front door and seated in his car.

'You'll tell me how you make out? And you'll put my side of it squarely before the cops?'

'Sure to both questions, Frank. And thanks for the dope. Oh, I just remembered. You don't have anybody following me around with the idea of keeping me on the hop?'

'Of course I haven't anybody following you. Mort mentioned it on the phone while you were on the way here. Who could it be?'

'Probably nothing but my guilty conscience,' Wayne grinned. He drove away from the house.

17

He watched for a car following him home to Vine Street, but saw nothing suspicious in the mirror. He had thought it might be a good idea to get in touch with Hank Petersen or Lieutenant Eckert at once and give them details of his interview with Frank Cotter, but then he thought it might be a better idea to sleep on what he had learned from the Cotter brothers.

He parked the Plymouth and lingered on the street for a few minutes in the shadows to see if anyone would drive along. Nobody did. He went up to his apartment, had a shower, made a drink and sat down at the TV.

Wayne often found that his problems kept churning around in his subconscious mind while he was doing something quite different from worrying about them. Often too a solution would pop out suddenly like the jackpot from a fruit machine. He watched a Western for half an hour and nothing happened. Finally he went to the phone and dialled Ruth Foran's number. Ruth was surprised to hear from him at this hour.

'Is something the matter, Joe?'

'Yeah, there is, honey. I've realised there's something missing from my day. I'd like to rest my head on your shoulder for an hour. It wouldn't appeal to you, huh?'

'I'll have an answer for you by the time you get here,' the girl said. 'Would that sort of compromise be acceptable?'

'Stand by for the man from Muddlesville,' he responded and switched off the TV.

It was two o'clock when he got back to Vine Street again.

He awakened early and was at the office early. He only intended to check the mail before continuing to headquarters for a talk with Hank Petersen. There was nothing much of interest in the mail, nothing but a few more free samples that Maggie had sent for.

'I've got to have some kicks out of life, Joe.'

'But after-shave lotion, honey? This is ridiculous.'

He was heading out again when the phone rang. It was Hank Petersen at the other end of the line when he answered it. Petersen sounded mildly excited.

'I've just had a call from Frank Cotter, Joe. He wanted to know if you'd been in touch with me last night.'

'What did he say?'

'He said what you've got to tell us is the truth. I suggested riding over for a share of the daylight. He says you've got it all. So what about it?'

'I'm on my way, Hank.'

'You'd better be, pal.'

Petersen was waiting when Wayne reached police headquarters. Floyd Eckert didn't seem to be around and for this Wayne was glad. Eckert would be cynical about Frank Cotter's story. He would probably see it as a smoke screen to shield the real truth of his part in Mitzi Laverick's murder.

Petersen didn't say a word until Wayne was through. Then he lit a cigarette and began pacing the office floor.

'It's just crazy enough to be true,' was his verdict presently. 'It jells too with what we know of the dame, Joe. She was a dame was fond of the guys. But if neither Frank nor Mort put this dark-skinned guy to tailing you, who did? Who is he, and why in hell is he trying to scare you off?'

'I've thought about it, Hank. I've come up with the notion that the guy is just too obvious to be real.'

Petersen frowned at him. 'How come? I'm not much at riddles so early in the day, Joe. You said he keeps warning you to lay off. He did flash a gun at you . . . '

'Mort Cotter flashed a gun at me. Mort was only kidding, as it turns out. Sometimes I pull a gun on somebody when I'm kidding. So do you, I bet.'

'Okay. But if he isn't trying to get you off the case, where's the point?'

'Let's say he's keeping in close touch, Hank. He knows that Mitzi hired me to get her out of town in one piece. He knows that Mitzi must have told me a little of her trouble to get me operating in the first place.'

'You figure he thinks you know more about her than you do?' Petersen suggested. 'I've got it, Joe. The dough! The money we found at her apartment . . .'

Wayne smiled faintly.

'Maybe we're getting some place at last. It's true that the guy followed me around the banks in town here. He followed me around the banks in Ashbury — '

'Sure! So why was he following you around the banks? To let you find the money for him, of course . . .'

Wayne looked sharply at Petersen.

'Who have you told about it, Hank?'

'You think we're amateurs? We've told nobody. If what Frank Cotter says is true, then the dough belongs to him. There's no danger of him giving the news to anybody.'

'Maybe not. Can I use the phone?'

Petersen nodded. He perched on his desk while Wayne got an outside line and contacted *Montcalm*. As it happened, Frank Cotter was at home. Wayne announced himself, then told Cotter to keep quiet about the money.

'I didn't intend doing anything else. Do you think you have a lead?'

'Your dough's safe, Frank, if that's what you mean. No, not really. Thanks for your co-operation.'

'But you said the dough is safe. What — '

'I'll explain later,' Wayne said and hung up.

Now an idea was coming to life in his mind. He didn't want to tell Petersen about it. Petersen gaped when he turned to the door of the office.

'Where do you think you're going? What's the tie-in with the guy who's been tailing you?'

'I want to mull it over, Hank. There isn't the right atmosphere in this joint for thinking. I'm going home to my office to do it.'

'Then you're giving the Cotters a clean bill of health?'

'That's up to your department, Hank. All I did was act like your stooge. From this on you'll have to form your own conclusions about the Cotters.'

He walked out before Petersen could find his tongue.

★ ★ ★

Back in his office Wayne called the number that Dell Lavers had left with him. It appeared that Lavers was still hanging around his apartment until something definite was brought to light regarding his sister's murder.

'Have you made any progress yet?' was his opening question when Wayne spoke to him.

'I'm not sure. Tell me, Dell, did you know that your sister got married shortly after she left New York?'

'What!'

Wayne held the phone away from his ear and looked at Maggie.

'The poor kid,' Maggie said. 'It must be a shock to him.'

'So you didn't know about the wedding, Dell?' Wayne said tautly when Lavers had calmed down.

'No, of course I didn't. It must be a mistake. It must — '

'You didn't know any guy she was friendly with when she left New York?'

'Nothing, I tell you. Nothing — '

'Thanks for the help,' Wayne murmured and hung up.

He lit a cigarette and stared at the window. Had he spent so much time following a false trail when the answer was so simple and so manifest from the word go?

'Can I get you a cup of coffee or an aspirin, Joey? You strike me like a guy was about to have a brain-storm or come out in a rash.'

'I'm all right, Maggie. Just let me stew. If I don't win the medal for prize dope of the year, then the cops are bound to get it.'

He was leaving the office again when the phone rang. He stood at the door while Maggie Yarmon answered it. Maggie lifted her head. She covered the mouthpiece.

'Dave Chalmers of the *Herald*. Looking for information, I bet. He says it's important. Will I tell him to make a disc?'

'I'd better talk with him.' Wayne sat on

the edge of the desk and took the receiver. 'This is me, Dave.'

'Sorry I couldn't dig up much on Frank Cotter, Joe,' Chalmers said. 'But I did find one interesting tit-bit.'

'What is it, Dave?' Wayne had a good idea what it would be. When newspaper men commenced digging they didn't go about it in a half-hearted manner.

'He and the canary in question were on pretty good terms,' Chalmers told him. 'Would that rate a lifted eye-brow in any quarters?'

'Not so you'd notice. It does confirm something I've already found out. Thanks a million.'

'Nothing sensational yet, Joe?'

Wayne detected a slight tremor in Chalmers's voice that set him wondering. He said carefully, 'Not really, Dave. But you're my favourite journalist, and — '

'Don't tell me. Okay, Joe, you don't rattle easy. But pin your ears back for a proper explosion.'

'She was married?' Wayne suggested.

'What do you know!' Chalmers snorted. 'Another damp squib. Joe, you're one guy doesn't need any help from me. Then you know she was married to — '

'You've found that out?' Wayne said excitedly. 'Dave, it's the piece that I'm looking for.'

'I'm glad something registers out of all my effort. She was married about six months ago to a guy called Jeremy Abbott — '

'Don't stop now, Dave. You've got me hanging on to the cliff with my fingernails. You know where Abbott is at?'

'Sorry. He's one of these guys that keeps flitting around. But I got a whisper he and the Laverick cutie pulled a couple of sharp deals while they rested up in Las Vegas.'

'Well, that's something, Dave.' Wayne tried to hide his disappointment. 'There's no description of Abbott available, I suppose?'

'Sure there is. I got a photo from our man on a Nevada newspaper. Would you like to see it?'

'Would I what! Dave, you're a real peach. What are you?'

'A peach,' Chalmers said. 'Surprise,

surprise. If you want the photograph I'll send it over there.'

'Right away?'

'You bet. It must be a month since a guy called me a peach. And I'll get a story maybe?'

'You bet. But not a word to anybody until it breaks, Dave.'

Chalmers grunted assent. Wayne hung up and ran a hand over his head. Maggie Yarmon noticed his excitement. She grinned and poked a cigarette at her lips.

'Some joy at last, Joey?'

'There might be, Maggie. Everything depends on this photograph being of the guy I think it is. If it turns out to be somebody else, it blows my cute theory to blazes.'

Fifteen minutes later the doorbell was pushed and Wayne found a messenger from the *Herald* waiting on the step. He gave the messenger five dollars and grabbed an envelope from his fingers. He closed the door and drew a photograph out of the envelope. The image that stared back at him was that of the dark-skinned man who had been following him around.

★　★　★

He spent the whole of the day searching for Jeremy Abbott. Nobody remembered having seen Abbott; nobody knew where a man called Jeremy Abbott lived.

It came to him that Abbott had learned of the police finding the money that Mitzi had hidden at her apartment on Comstock Avenue, and was now well clear of Darton City before the police finally tumbled to him. If this was so, it was Wayne's duty to contact Hank Petersen at once and tell him everything he knew, including his theory regarding the murder. He decided to hold on for another day at least. The police had as much of the picture as he had, and there were enough brains at headquarters to work it out for themselves.

In the evening he drove to Comstock Avenue on the off-chance of the owner of the apartment house where Mitzi Laverick had lived recalling Jeremy Abbott visiting. The manager of the apartment house was in evidence. He was a middle-aged man and didn't mind talking with Wayne. No, he said, he never knew Miss Laverick to have visitors of any kind.

Wayne asked if he might look at the room where the girl lived. It was impossible. Another tenant had taken up residence. The police had given him permission. Anyhow, the police had searched the apartment from floor to ceiling. Wayne said thanks and left. He should have gone to the apartment house in the first place. He may or may not have found the money, but he would hardly have uncovered anything else that the police had overlooked.

He was driving through the shadows on Comstock Avenue when he realised that a car was following him.

To make sure the car was following him he drove in and out of a number of side streets. The car cruised in his wake everywhere he went, keeping what the driver probably thought was a safe distance. When Wayne directed the Plymouth across town he had one good look at the car under bright lights. It was the grey Ford, he was certain. Jeremy

Abbott was apparently still interested in his movements.

On a hunch Wayne set out for the direction of the Wilton Buildings. He pulled up at the front of the buildings and lit a cigarette before locking the Plymouth and taking the elevator to his offices.

In Maggie Yarmon's office he switched on the light and left the door off the lock. He had dangled pretty obvious bait, to be sure, but wasn't Jeremy Abbott a pretty obvious character, and shouldn't he have been able to see through him the first time he came in contact with him?

Wayne brought a bottle and paper cup to Maggie's chair and sat down on it. He swallowed a drink, threw the cup at the waste basket, and lit a cigarette. He had his .38 under the edge of the desk when the door opened gently and the dark-faced man peered in.

'Ah! You're here, Mr. Wayne . . . '

Wayne pretended surprise until the other had taken a step inside the office. He closed the door with his heel and pointed the Colt automatic at Wayne's chest.

'Sure I'm here,' Wayne said thinly. 'I figured you'd gotten over your crush on me and found somebody else to tag around after. And if you've any sense at all in your skull you'll point that gun at yourself, Jeremy.'

At mention of the name the man's eyelids flickered. A cold smile warped his lips.

'So you know who I am? You've persisted until you found out I was Mitzi's husband. A lot of good it's going to do you, shamus.' He moved cautiously to a chair opposite Wayne and sat down. He made a motion with the automatic. 'I'd rather see your hands in full view, mister. Place them on the desk.'

Wayne let the .38 slip to his lap and stretched his arms on top of the desk. He killed his cigarette in the tray.

'I know plenty about you, Jeremy. I know plenty about your wife too. You and she were a couple of sharks. Or should I call you birds of a feather . . . '

Abbott's forehead corrugated in a slight frown. 'You get more intriguing every time I see you, Wayne. But I did warn you to lay off — '

'You warned me all right, Jeremy. But you were pulling a bluff a yard wide. You followed me around to see what I was up to, then you gave me an odd jab in the tail to keep me on the hop. What kind of perch did you think I'd land on finally, pal — the twenty-four thousand bucks?'

Abbott rocked visibly on his chair. Sweat oozed to his brow and he took a handkerchief from his pocket to wipe it away. When he spoke again his voice was a hoarse rasp.

'I wondered if Cotter told you about the money, Wayne. Or was it Mitzi who told you about it? It's what I want, pal. I've put up with a lot to get my hands on that sort of dough.'

'Sure you have, chum. Including murder. You pretended you wanted me out of your hair while all the time you hoped I would make like an eager beaver until the money came to light . . . '

The man's eyes glinted. He ran his tongue over his lips. 'You really have the money, Wayne? You know where it is?'

'I know where it is.'

'You've got it?' He leaned forward on his chair. 'You have it hidden?'

'Don't be stupid, Jeremy. I didn't get into this gag for peanuts. I had a hunch right from the start what was in the wind. Stop me where I go wrong. You laid your wife as bait for Frank Cotter in Vegas. You got her to play hard to get for a while to whet Cotter's appetite up. When Mitzi appeared to succumb to Cotter's charm she gave him a line about you wanting money to grant a divorce. How much were you planning to take him for, Jeremy?'

Abbott touched his lips with his tongue again.

'Thirty thousand bucks,' he said slowly. 'Mitzi and I didn't really hit it off as marriage partners. All she wanted was money and fun. All I wanted was the dough.'

'Do you know how much she got from Cotter?'

'She kept putting me off. She said Cotter wasn't keen on paying. She was a liar. I know she got a load of dough out of him. I told her I would tell Cotter if she didn't split fifty-fifty the way we planned.'

'What did she say to that?'

'She said I hadn't the nerve. She said I'd land in jail if I showed my nose near Cotter.'

'Did you know she planned on taking off without you?'

'Sure I knew. I was watching her like a hawk. She bought a new car. She said if I'd leave her alone to get to where she was going, she'd mail my share to me.'

'That was when you planned to murder her, Jeremy?'

'You can't prove anything, Wayne. All I want is the dough. Help me to get it and I'll pay you a thousand.'

'You figured she was taking the dough out in the car, pal. You filed the studs so there'd be an accident. You tailed the car out of town so you could grab the dough when it happened. Things didn't pan out to your liking. That motorcycle cop spoiled your play — '

'Not so you'd notice, smart guy. I was right behind the car when it went through the fence. I parked and searched while you were in dreamland. I thought you were dead. If I'd thought you were alive I'd have finished you there and then. I used gloves to search. She had four or five hundred in her purse. The loot wasn't stashed in the car. I left her purse alone in case it queered up the pitch. I went down the road again and turned. That was when I saw the cop.'

Wayne's mouth hardened as he considered him. He had been right after all. The solution to the problem had been under his nose the whole of the time. It just went to show. Mitzi wanted all of the money for herself. She had hired him to see her safely out of town. The money was safe where she had left it, she thought. Then, when Abbott had given up and gone away she would have returned. She might even have gone back to Frank Cotter. Wayne wondered if Abbott knew about the baby. He didn't ask him. He couldn't bring himself to ask him. He would like to know how and when Abbott had worked at the wheel studs of the Dodge. It was something for Petersen and Eckert to find out when they had Abbott at headquarters.

How was he going to get him to headquarters?

'But you haven't got the dough, Jeremy. And you know something, chum, I'll bet a five-spot to a nickel that you never get it.'

Abbott stood up and levelled the Colt. A sneer gathered at his lips.

'Why do you think I've stuck with you, shamus? Either you help me to get it and collect your thousand or — '

The phone at Wayne's elbow rang.

It caused Wayne to start slightly. It brought a frown to Abbott's olive-skinned features.

'Who is it?'

'How do I know? Could be my secretary.'

'Yeah! And it could be the cops . . . '

Wayne shrugged when the phone rang again, for longer this time.

'I don't answer it and somebody's going to investigate why I don't.'

'Okay, shamus. Answer it. But one word out of place — '

'Don't have a stroke. I get the message.'

Wayne picked up the receiver. Hank

Petersen barked in his ear. 'I've been trying to raise you, Joe. I tried your apartment. I tried your secretary, then your girl-friend . . . '

'What's the matter?'

'Lashlin just remembered where he had seen that dark-faced guy before, Joe. He warned him about parking with no lights. We're at his apartment now to check him out. He isn't here. But here is the payoff, Joe . . . '

Wayne said, 'Yeah?'

'His name is Jeremy Abbott. That Mitzi Laverick dame was married to a guy called Abbott. We've been tracing him all over the place.'

'No kidding?'

'What the hell do you mean, no kidding?' Petersen snapped. 'Aren't you interested? Are you going to help find this guy?'

'I'm sorry, lady. It's after hours for me. Come to my office first thing in the morning and we'll talk about it.'

'Joe!' Petersen raged. 'Have you gone crazy?'

Wayne hung up and grinned at Abbott.

Abbott was leaning towards the desk, sweat glistening on his brow.

'Who was it?' he rasped suspiciously.

'An old lady. She wants me to trace somebody for her.'

'It didn't sound like an old lady.'

'So what? She gave me her phone number. I can ring her back and let you talk with her.'

Jeremy Abbott stood off a little. He was bringing his handkerchief from his pocket again when Wayne caught the edge of the desk and hurled it outwards.

A lot of things happened during the next few seconds. Phone, typewriter, notepads went flying. The typewriter struck Abbott on the leg and threw him backwards. The gun in his hand roared and a bullet slapped into the wall at Wayne's back. Wayne spun with his .38 in his fingers, bullets spewing out of it at the dark-skinned man. They were all aimed low, or as near to low as Wayne could manage in the circumstances.

Scream after scream came from Jeremy Abbott as he floundered on the office floor. Wayne stepped to him and kicked the Colt automatic aside. He propped Abbott in a corner to keep him upright and then brought him a drink. He had shot the man three times in the legs and thigh. He was trying to get a paper cup to his mouth when he fainted.

He lit a cigarette and went to the phone on the floor. He gathered it up and got through to police headquarters.

'Send an ambulance to my office in the Wilton Buildings,' he said flatly. 'Then get news to Petersen or Lieutenant Eckert. I've got Jeremy Abbott here.'

He was making bandages for the wound in Abbott's thigh when Hank Petersen stormed through the door.

THE END

We do hope that you have enjoyed reading this large print book.

Did you know that all of our titles are available for purchase?

We publish a wide range of high quality large print books including:

Romances, Mysteries, Classics General Fiction Non Fiction and Westerns

Special interest titles available in large print are:

The Little Oxford Dictionary Music Book, Song Book Hymn Book, Service Book

Also available from us courtesy of Oxford University Press:

Young Readers' Dictionary (large print edition) Young Readers' Thesaurus (large print edition)

For further information or a free brochure, please contact us at:
**Ulverscroft Large Print Books Ltd., The Green, Bradgate Road, Anstey, Leicester, LE7 7FU, England.
Tel:** (00 44) **0116 236 4325
Fax:** (00 44) **0116 234 0205**

THE HARASSED HERO

Ernest Dudley

Murray Selwyn, six-foot-two and athletic, was so convinced he had not long to live that when he came across a hold-up, a murder and masses of forged fivers, he was too worried about catching a chill to give them much attention. But when he met his pretty nurse, Murray began to forget his ailments, and by the end of a breath-taking chase after some very plausible crooks, the hypochondriac had become a hero.

HELL HATH NO FURY

Rex Marlowe

Private investigator Sam Spain receives a visit from a little old lady, who wants him to find her twenty-two-year-old daughter, Irene, who has been missing for a month. Sam learns that Hugo Dare, a racketeer-turned-politician, has supplied Irene with a bungalow on Eucalyptus Drive. From the moment Sam discovers a corpse in Irene's room, he runs into nothing but grief. Irene is in a jam, framed for murder. Sam hides the girl and goes on with his investigation. Then he finds himself in the same jam as Irene — framed for a murder he hasn't committed!

A LONELY PLACE TO DIE

Colin Robertson

'The old lady — with a bustle.' These words, uttered by Vincent Stroud before he was murdered, set Peter Gayleigh once again on the adventure trail. He becomes interested in a remote castle in Scotland where something very odd appears to be going on. His determination to solve this mystery brings him into contact with Shirley Quentin whose father, the owner of the castle, has disappeared. Finally, on a Scottish moor, Gayleigh meets the Herr Doktor Ulrich von Shroeder, a biochemist and master spy.